Socrates

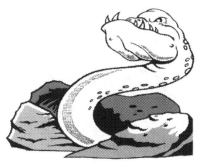

Uncle Gnarls

Poker

Bondar

Amaya

Noni

Serine

Little Peetie

Zippee

Kaihula

Jacko

Shredder

Two Stars

Tooney and Schooner

Baaya

Big Jake

Jazzy

Ka'e'a'e'a

Kaimana

Captain Sam O'brien

Ms Joleen Teal

Kabooga

Nuimalu

Keapualani

Chloe

Kooks

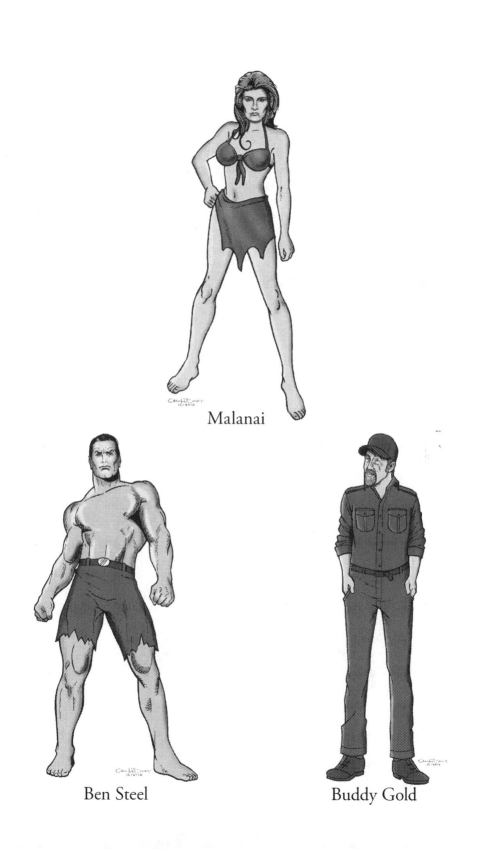

Malanai

Ben Steel

Buddy Gold

Jibber

Stony and Rocky

Acknowledgments

I want to thank my dear wife, Robin, for her loving support and professional insight. What a joy to have spent 40 years of marriage navigating life at each other's side.

A special note of thanks goes to Cecil Highley of Louisville, Kentucky, a dear friend and exceptional artist. Cecil's cover art and illustrations throughout the entire Socrates' Wild Ocean Adventure series are a crucial element in bringing the story and characters to life. I would also like to thank Cecil's grandson, Zack Allen, for his artistic assistance.

A heartfelt thank you to another aspiring young artist on the island of Maui, Jeremy Rivera, whose illustration of a large seahorse stallion helped develop the cover art for this book.

My wife and I would also like to thank Ms. Flecha Tovar, Hawaii's representative for Ms. America 2015. Flecha approved of us using her photo … that of a true Apache Princess, to capture the essence of the dynamic character 'Malanai' in this work. Congratulations on your recent achievements and we wish you success for your future.

We are also very appreciative to the Choctaw Nation of Oklahoma's Language Department for helping translate some of the dialogue into the Choctaw language. 'Yakoke' to Dora Wickson and staff for your support.

Battle for Atlantis

Book 4: Socrates' Adventure Continues

Thomas McGee

authorHOUSE®

AuthorHouse™
1663 Liberty Drive
Bloomington, IN 47403
www.authorhouse.com
Phone: 1 (800) 839-8640

Published by AuthorHouse   09/08/2015

ISBN: 978-1-5049-2074-2 (sc)
ISBN: 978-1-5049-2107-7 (hc)
ISBN: 978-1-5049-2108-4 (e)

Contents

Chapter 1

Racing to the helm, Joleen shouted; "Corey, what is *going on?*"

"Check the screen and scroll back two minutes."

Joleen's eyes opened wide; "Are those destroyers?"

"Yep; they are Los Angeles class and preparing for a fight. Before we submerged, I also picked up a satellite image of four F16s heading our way. I think our effort to mimic the solar flare triggered a military reaction."

"He's right Joleen," James added; "After our laser tests over North Korea and Iran, the military has to be on high alert."

Joleen turned to Corey; "So, what do we do?"

"All I know is that we cannot draw attention to the area surrounding the caverns. We have to lead them at least fifty miles away and create some sort of diversion."

Charlie suddenly piped up with an idea; "Joseph, get the map and find the nearest deep-water trench. We need a place to hide."

In a panic Corey called out; "We've got another problem! Look at the monitor!" Coming up on the screen was a huge cargo ship. "Is it my imagination or is that ship painted totally ... black?"

The crew focused intently on the ghastly vessel. It was at least a hundred miles off the normal route for cargo ships. Using an image enhancer, Corey zoomed in for a closer look. There was something eerily strange about the ship, no cargo being visible and not low enough in the water for an obvious payload. Its arbitrary serpentine course tipped the vessel's identity off to Joseph Hawk, his face taking on a stone-cold glare: *"It's the Mother Ship!"*

No one questioned his statement; it made perfect sense. The pirate speedboat they confronted earlier could not be cruising around hundreds of miles offshore without any resources available to re-fuel. This massive ship had to be a floating headquarters for the pirates' activities. Engaging the cloaking scanner, Corey quickly honed in on their precise distance to the ship: "Three miles; there are only three miles separating us: Any Ideas?"

Charlie pointed to a spot on the map and took charge: "Use a sonar ping to verify distance to the ship and head for that trench. Stay close to the surface and put the pedal to the metal. Let's hope we get chased."

"What about the destroyers," asked Corey?

"I'm working on it," answered Charlie. Then turning to James he said, "I've got some calculating to do; go to the Raptor's control room and I will meet you there in a minute. Joseph, Carlynn, when we approach the trench search out a hiding place, a crevice, anything. Corey, you and Joleen do whatever you have to do to keep that Mother Ship fixated on us. Then, when we reach the trench, verify distance to the lead destroyer with another ping."

"But Sir," Corey responded, "that will be a sure sign they are being targeted!"

"I'm counting on it," smiled Charlie.

The Mother Ship responded quickly to the sonar ping, a large hatch opening on its starboard side allowing for the instantaneous launch of three sleek craft from their perches, hitting the water at high speed. Each were equipped with two deck mounted fifty caliber machine guns as well as crews of armed men in dark, tattered clothing. The boats were individually fitted with five two-hundred-fifty horsepower outboard engines, making their speed overwhelming. There was absolutely no way for Nations Pride to outrun them, however, it did have the advantage of invisibility, the capacity to dive to any depth, and the maneuverability of a stealth fighter. As the speedboats closed in on their location, Corey mumbled; "You want to play cat and mouse? We'll give you cat and mouse!" Veering off course he said to Charlie; "Sir, I've got this."

Charlie had no problem letting the helmsman have his way. Corey turned back toward the speedboats using Captain O'Brien's' strategy. Within forty-five seconds, the boats raced over Nations Pride and began fanning out to maximize their search for the source of the sonar signal. Corey then began following one of them. At intervals of fifteen seconds, he kept re-directing a sonar ping back to the Mother Ship, causing mass confusion among the speedboat operators.

Responding to the mayhem Corey was causing on the surface, Charlie raced into the Raptor's control room, instructing James; "It's time we get our bird in the sky."

The staff on Joleen Teal's private island had everything prepared. After the Raptors' earlier flight over the canyon, the maintenance crew had the craft ready to fly again within minutes of its return to home base.

"Charlie called out over the intercom, "Corey, verify distance to the destroyers!" Then, taking a deep breath, he mumbled, "I sure hope the Mother Ship is unaware of the Navy's presence."

Corey curiously responded; "What is it you have in mind, Sir?"

Charlie answered, "We, my young friend, are going to light up that Mother Ship like a roman candle. It may be our ticket to maneuvering everyone away from the canyon."

Charlie's eyes suddenly opened wide; "Oh shoot!" Racing from the control room he quickly asked Joleen; "The window in the cavern closed, didn't it?"

In tears she replied, "Yes, Charlie; I am so sorry. I did not know how to tell you and Carlynn."

Charlie's smile grew wide, clasping his hands around Joleen's' face and kissing her on the forehead, blurting out; "Lady, you are an *Angel.*"

Sprinting back to the control room, Charlie spun his chair around, sat down, and told James: "It's time to play."

Transmitting co-ordinates to the Raptor's computer, the hypersonic aircraft was airborne in seconds. Speaking with Corey on his headset, Charlie started directing every move: "Helmsman, bring us aft, crank 'er to thirty-five knots, dive and level us off at fifty fathoms; head straight for the Mother Ship."

Corey was curious as to how they were going to signal the Raptor from that depth. Yet, he had total confidence in Charlie's prowess.

It took only minutes for Nations Pride to pass under the bow of the enormous vessel. When directly under center Charlie called out, "Stop and verify distance to the lead destroyer with another ping."

The crew onboard the Mother Ship was panicking, being unable to identify the source of the transmission. After passing under the ships' stern, Charlie calmly instructed; "Seaman Coulson, bring us up to six fathoms."

Reaching the six-fathom mark, Charlie began counting down … "Five, four, three, two, and one---Fire!"

Light from the Raptor's laser streaked through the sky, the resulting molecular disruption with the helm of the Mother Ship lighting it up with the glow of a nuclear blast, causing it to shake violently. The frightened crew was scurrying around in complete chaos, most seeking their escape by leaping into the ocean. The destroyers distance from the incident actually shielded the lights source from its effect. By the time the Navy vessels could respond, the Raptor was speeding back to Ms. Teal's Island. Charlie now directed Corey; "Get us to the trench and tuck us in. Let's see what happens."

The destroyers were plowing through the water full tilt when one of the speedboats made a fatal mistake, launching a rocket propelled grenade at one of the ships. The military's countermeasures, coupled with a flurry of shelling, dispatched the incoming ordinance and all three boats in seconds. The destroyers then addressed the mysteriously glowing Mother Ship, and upon identifying the maverick vessel, ordered their four F16 escorts to 'cut 'er down', the attack splitting the vessel in half from bow to stern, sinking it in less than a minute. The Navy then launched life rafts, plucking survivors of the outlaw crew from the water. All onboard Nations Pride watched the monitor, wondering what would happen next. Charlie came up with another idea: "Corey, get fifteen miles separation; we are going to send a message."

As Nations Pride neared the fifteen-mile mark, Charlie transmitted a message in Morse code ... "A gift from Seal Team Six."

The appreciative Commanders of both destroyers did not question the transmission, ordering their crews to attention on the bows of their respective ships, followed by a salute into the Atlantic's vast empty expanse. Then, with their captives locked away, both ships set course for the mainland.

While the crew aboard Nations Pride watched the monitor, silently awaiting the destroyers to disappear into the distance, Joseph Hawks' face took on an ear-to-ear grin. With his massive arms locked across his chest, he leaned back, whispering to Charlie, "Mmmm ... Good trick."

Charlie replied, "Yeah, well, it may not play out so well when they find out that Seal Team Six was nowhere near this area today. We have to get back to the island and come up with a plan to recover our crew as well as a way to keep the military as far away as possible from our discovery. Believe me, there will be a swift response to this little episode and we cannot waste our time running interference."

Chapter 2

Captain Sam O'Brien, Chloe, and Buddy floated helplessly through the hollow corridor of inner space, their journey ending in a gentle plunge into the pristine waters of a magnificent cavern, Socrates and his companions splashing down right beside them. There, ready to greet them, was none other than Tooney and Schooner, the youngster blurting out, *"Follow me!"*

Sam, Chloe, and Buddy quickly complied, frantically trying to keep up, while Socrates and his friends positioned themselves close behind. Baaya, of course, could not keep silent: "We just got here! Why are we in a *hurry?* Hello, is anybody *listening?* Like, can we just *slow down?*" No one paid her any attention.

It took only a few moments for Tooney and Schooner to lead the divers to the beach fronting the bay where the other humans were gathered. As Sam, Chloe, and Buddy began removing their dive masks, their faces suddenly took on a look of wonder, seeing several dozen people on shore huddling together, their scant clothing, coupled with fresh wounds, giving evidence of a recent scrape with death. Ben Steel and his companions took a defensive posture, ready to do battle with those exiting the water, a spark of fear gripping them over the strange apparel worn by the divers. Sam hackled up, putting his arm out and quickly pulling Chloe behind him while shouting an inquiry to the crowd gathered on the shore: *"Is there any chance that one of you is Anders Highley?"*

Leaping to his feet, one young man ran up to Sam confidently responding; "Yes Sir, I am Anders Highley. Do I know you?"

Sam gazed into the eyes of a young man who appeared in his early twenties. This situation made no sense, the last Bermuda Triangle tragedy having happened many decades ago. Sam then noticed that most all present were relatively young, none older than maybe their mid thirties. Sam took a moment before asking Anders, "Young man, how long ago did you last transmit a distress signal?"

"Why, only moments ago, sir. We managed to escape our captors and I was finally able to retrieve my radio. I could not believe that it is still in such good condition."

Sam replied, "How long have you been here son?"

"I do not know sir. We have never been able to calculate time in this place. All any of us have known since arriving here is the extreme condition of our captivity."

Ben Steel motioned for his friends to stand down, kindly offering the newcomers some hospitality: "Please, feel free to take off your equipment and have a seat. By the way, I am Ben, Ben Steel." Turning to Malanai he asked; "Sweetheart, would you mind rounding up some fruit and water for our guests? We have a lot to explain to, oh I am sorry; your name, Sir?"

Sam smiled, "I am retired Navy Captain Sam O'Brien, and this is my daughter Chloe, as well as my old friend, also retired from the military, Major Buddy Gold. The little boy you see riding the dolphin in the bay is the one who is responsible for bringing us here: his name is Tooney. We are part of a team exploring recent events in the Bermuda Triangle and we just happened to pick up a distress call from Aviator Highley."

Ben's eyes lit up: "You mean our signal worked?"

Buddy replied, "The signal was faint, but Anders' skills at Morse code are what brought us here. I am impressed."

"So," continued Ben, "does this mean we can go home?"

Sam took a moment, accepting a curled base of a palm frond full of sparkling water from Malanai and taking a sip before continuing: "That is something we are working on. Unfortunately, we have a few details to work out."

Anders turned to the rest of the captives, joyfully shouting out, *"We will be going home soon; these guys are here to take us home."* The entire group began hugging each other in triumph.

Sam motioned Ben over to a private place: "Um, uh, I do not wish to rain on your parade, but, this rescue could take awhile. It is a logistics problem."

Ben looked confused at Sam's use of the strange term, logistics. "Sir, I do not understand."

Sam then asked, "What was the date of the tragedy that brought you here Ben?"

"Our plane went down on July eighteenth, Sir. Anders was working on his skill as a pilot and he asked me to accompany him as navigator. Suddenly, a horrific storm engulfed us and an enormous circle of fire flashed up from the ocean, an overwhelming force pulling us into the flames. Anders managed to keep it together and flatten out our landing. We scurried to get out of the plane as it began sinking, frantically swimming away and ending up in a glowing underwater cavern where there just happened to be a pocket of breathable air. We rested for about an hour before noticing the intense golden glow slowly subsiding. We hurriedly started exploring the cavern and found something really strange: a vertical wall of shimmering, watery sunshine, giving the appearance of a way back to the surface. The growing darkness in the cavern enforced our decision to take, what we thought, our only way out. We jumped in … not realizing the consequences."

Sam sat spellbound as Ben continued his explanation of the captives' plight right up to their recent rescue. While continuing to listen to Ben's story, the Captain stood up, staring out into the shallows only to see Socrates watching the goings on onshore. The Captain winked at Socrates … and Socrates winked back. Sam yielded to this surreal experience. He was finally beginning to understand Tooneys connection with his dolphin friend. Joleen had touched on the subject back on her island; 'in the absence of fear, there is profound unity'.

Wrapping up his narrative, Ben concluded; "Sir, I am really looking forward to going home and seeing my family. What is today's date?"

Sam hesitantly replied, "Today is ... September fifteenth."

Ben quickly leaped to his feet, "What, Anders and I have only been gone a couple of months? It seems much longer than that. But, oh well, I am sure my mom will be happy that I am still alive."

Sam hesitated for a moment before asking Ben his next question: "Young man, you mentioned the date July eighteenth; what year was that?"

"Why, it was this year sir; nineteen forty-five."

The young man was oblivious to the reality that some seven decades had passed since he had seen his family.

Sam felt sickened by the fact that these dear people were excitedly looking forward to going home, back to an unrecognizable world where conditions are far more complex than what they left behind. The basic simplicity of life, along with the innocence and human dignity that were generally intact in earlier decades are a thing of the past, aside from the fact that most all of their known relatives would by now be asleep in their graves. Sam decided it would be best to get some rest before starting a history lesson. These lost souls deserved to hear the truth before embarking on a plan to return them to face a mixed up modern society that would prove to be beyond a doubt, a terrible disappointment.

Chapter 3

Socrates retreated into deeper water, the humans having settled in farther from the shoreline. Jazzy was busy trying to settle Baaya down, the little angelfish still complaining over having to hurry to follow Tooney and Schooner. Growing tired of her constant fussing, Uncle Gnarls offered the girls a suggestion: "Zippee, Serine, and Two Stars, why don't you take our newcomers out to the mouth of the bay for something to eat? I am sure some *delicious shrimp* would be a welcome treat."

Auntie Noni's brow popped up like a loaded spring; *"Gnarls!"*

With a crooked smile on his face he replied, "Ah honey, I am just trying to be hospitable."

Turning to Noni with a smirk on her face Baaya piped in, "Yeah, what is wrong with a little hospitality, *hmmm?*"

Noni's demeanor changed in an instant: "Oh, I am sorry sweetheart; this little one is apparently famished."

Peetie then had Schooner race Tooney to the shore to drop him off so that the little dolphin could join the feast. Peetie winked at Uncle Gnarls, stating in a whisper; "Uncle, the dolphins need to eat too. And what about your son and family, they also missed out on the last scrumptious feast."

Gnarls smiled and joined in rounding up all the fish to the location of the shrimp laden kelp, Poker and Kaimana taking the lead in introducing the recent arrivals to a meal they would not soon forget.

Jibber was reluctant when approaching the kelp but chomped right down when he saw the enormous numbers of shrimp lining the swaying plants. Then, joining in one by one, all began voraciously attacking the plants. Baaya was the first to finish her meal, being the smallest of the group. In addition, as usual, she could not keep her mouth shut, rolling up one of her fins, pulling it to her side and shouting, "Well, it is *about time!*"

However, only a couple of seconds later her face took on a troubled look, frantically searching for a place to escape, her tummy convulsing from a sudden surge of pent up gas, when … Blooop, blooo, blooo, blooo, blooo, bloop, the overwhelming rapid expulsion sending her spinning through the water like a pinwheel. Unable to control it she began crying out, "What is going on? Please, *help me!*"

Laughter rumbled through the bay, Jazzy and the dolphins quickly realizing they were having a trick played on them. Yet, they just rolled with it, buckling up and letting 'er rip'. Gnarls and Noni were laughing so hard they rolled up in a tight ball, which ended up being a mistake, Bohunk and his little ones wiggling in and blowing them apart. The dolphins decided to dive to the bottom of the bay and turning upward, picking up as much speed as possible, let the gas go just as they leaped out of the water, sending them a few feet higher than normal. Even though they had been through this before, Socrates and his friends could not resist the urge to join in. Little Peetie, Kaimana, and Ka'e'a'e'a joined Bohunks little ones in playing hide and seek. Of course, the bubbles were always giving away someone's position. Poker let go one so big that Baaya was engulfed by it, floating her upwards, and actually lifting her out of the water before popping. Her re-entry was not graceful, neither was she amused; but everyone else was laughing his or her heads off. The party continued unabated until the effect of the plants and shrimp subsided.

Gnarls, Noni, and Bohunk could not stop laughing. Stammering from his chuckle, Gnarls asked his son; "Do you re-re-remember when you were little and we used to swim to the surface and look up at the clouds and tr-tr-try and figure out what they resembled?"

Bohunk could hardly respond, but finally managed, "Y-y-yeah."

Gnarls asked, "D-d-d-did the bubbles remind you of anything you have seen before?"

Trying to catch his breath Bohunk replied, "W-w-w-w-well, I think my m-m-mate just let go a … s-salmon."

Exploding in laughter Gnarl's replied, "Yeah, I saw it, fins and everything."

The entire group of friends could not remember a laugh fest like this one. Eventually making their way back into shallower water they spent a significant amount of time telling stories of their lives and their favorite adventures. Of course, the exploits of Socrates and Poker dominated most of the conversation.

Chapter 4

"What do you mean, *Seal Team Six?* Seal Team Six is currently dealing with terrorists, not *Pirates!* You are talking to someone who knows that team's whereabouts 24/7 commander! I want an audience with the Joint Chiefs and the President within the hour; *got that!*"

Admiral McCauley's debriefing with Atlantic Fleet Command set him off on a violent tirade. His demand was a bit unusual because he was currently retired from official military operations. However, his overpowering reluctance to yield his command still struck fear in the hearts of most Top Brass. No one, but no one, dared question his seniority. He prided himself on his ability to stay in the loop when National security was threatened and that included his strategic advisory over the command of Seal Team Six. Slamming the phone down on his desk and seething with disgust he spun around in his chair and, leaping to his feet, immediately sprinted to a 3-D simulator in the far corner of his enormous office, typing in the co-ordinates of the Military's interception of the pirate vessel. The image produced was breathtaking, a complete topographical map of thousands of square miles of ranges and trenches below the ocean's surface. His mind began flooding with memories of strange events and tragedies claiming a significant loss of life in the Bermuda Triangle. After several tense moments, the scowl on his face began slowly subsiding, his shoulders slumping while hanging his head in shame, realizing his stubborn pride caused him to lose one of the very best professional relationships he had known in his life. Sam O'Brien had always proved himself a true friend and had simply asked for help regarding a map. It was not Sam's fault that a fugitive priest slipped through the cracks, managing to posture himself into an influential, albeit totally hypocritical, clerical appointment with the military. A tear came to the Admiral's eye, remembering that Sam's own nephew had been one of the priests' victims. He thought for a moment, sitting down in a chair while clasping his head in his hands, whispering; "What have I become?" Re-gathering his composure, he summoned Lieutenant Christopher: "Lieutenant, I need you to find Captain O'Brien. Also, connect me with the FBI. I need to talk to James Powell. Make it quick; I have some, uh, well … apologizing to do."

The Lieutenant was shocked; his boss's inability to apologize to anyone for anything was well known, stubborn pride never permitting a show of what he considered weakness. Yet, the Admiral's request brought a smile of relief and quick response from the young man.

However, after two hours of phone calls with the FBI and the security authority aboard the Ocean Gem, the Lieutenant's search yielded nothing. The Admiral sounded a bit perturbed by the failure to perform what should have been a simple task in that span of time. His voice was stern over the intercom: "Well, Lieutenant, *where are they?*"

"Sorry Sir, no clue sir; it's as if they dropped off the map."

"No one disappears into thin air, Lieutenant!"

"Well Sir, they are nowhere to be found. I have tried every resource we have and they seem to have just---vanished."

The Admiral briefly retreated, wondering if Sam and James' disappearances were somehow connected. He had an idea: "Lieutenant, request from Port Authority all surveillance tapes from the moment the Ocean Gem limped into dry dock up until this very moment. We need to start piecing this puzzle together."

The Port Authority complied with the Admiral's request without hesitation and the search was on. Scrolling through the first few days of video recording revealed nothing out of the ordinary. However, on one particular morning, young Tooney arrived with his parents, the three leaving later that evening. They returned the following morning, the little boy and Captain O'Brien getting in a vehicle and driving away only minutes before their arrival at the Admiral's secret meeting. The next thirty minutes were uneventful until Sam and Tooney's return to the dock, the Captain's face steaming with anger. Fast forwarding through the next several hours of files, FBI Agent James Powell suddenly arrived with an entourage of agents in five dark SUVs, picking up Captain O'Brien and Tooney before driving away. Forty-five minutes later James Powell departed after dropping Captain O'Brien and Tooney back off at the dock, Sam's face showing a look of relief. The Admiral suddenly started to choke up, the next day revealing the arrival of one of his and Sam's oldest friends, Buddy Gold. A few hours later, Buddy left the ship only to return the next day with an incredibly beautiful woman, the two arriving in a cream colored Bentley clad in gold trim. She departed within only a couple of hours. However, that same day Agent Powell returned, followed by the woman's pulling up in front of the ship less than an hour later in a stretch Hummer limousine. Luggage was quickly loaded into the back as Sam, Chloe, James, Buddy, Tooney, and his parents got in the vehicle and sped away. The file revealed no further presence of any of these individuals from that day forward. The Admiral engaged his young lieutenant, "What are they up to? Go to your desk and request information from the Cape's flight tower. See if any party accompanied by Captain O'Brien or Buddy Gold departed on the date noted on the camera."

"I will get right on it, Sir."

The reply came only moments later; "Nothing, Sir. There is, however, a sudden appearance and departure of a Desault Falcon 900, the flight list showing only one pilot accompanied by seven passengers. The flight co-ordinates are vague; somewhere in the Bahamas, the pilot claiming immunity from revealing final destination stating, 'Sovereign privilege of the Choctaw Nation.'"

The Admiral fired back, *"What in the world is going on?"*

Lieutenant Christopher replied, "Permission to speak freely Sir."

"What is on your mind young man?"

"Well Sir, it seems to me there are some dots to be connected. First, Captain O'Brien comes to you for help with a map, next you two have a major blowout which ends up with the FBI's involvement. Next, Sam has a meeting with Buddy Gold and the woman in the Bentley, followed by James Powell's return, etc., etc. Now, think about what was happening on the world scene only about a month after their disappearance. North Korea and Iran have sudden incidents that resemble nuclear explosions, yet no damage occurs. A few days later a similar incident happens in the Bermuda Triangle. Here is where it gets interesting; nowhere on earth is there an indication of the source of these events with the exception of a phantom message from Seal Team Six following the military's attack on a pirate ship that they say temporarily lit up like an exploding star before they fired on it, splitting it in two. Sir, I am thinking; perhaps you ought to call off the meeting with the President and the Joint Chiefs until we do more research on our own. Sam O'Brien's integrity is far above reproach, and if he came to you for help and found himself having to fall back on alternative resources---well, I am just saying--- perhaps he and young Tooney are really on to something."

The Admiral walked around the room for a moment, carefully weighing the significance of the young sailor's observations. He then sat back down, gazing at the flawed equation he and his team of advisors were working on, the formula still frozen in chalk on a huge archaic green board, an antiquated tool of the past which of itself revealed his stubborn pride, refusing to let go one of the last vestiges of his old school ways and yield to the efficiency of computers. However, after a few quiet moments, his eyes squinted tightly, recalling young Tooneys response to a mere glance at the equation and his subsequent giggling. The Admiral's eyes then opened wide, turning to the Lieutenant and blurting out: "That *young rascal* figured it out! What else could prompt Sam to recruit Buddy Gold, James Powell, and the others to leave so suddenly? That little guy solved a problem that elite scientific minds have been working on for over twenty years. And all it took him was a mere glance." After taking a deep breath he continued, "Lieutenant, I am going to clear you to accompany me on classified leave for an undetermined period of time. We are spinning our wheels with all of these so-called 'chosen advisors' the government has saddled us with. We have to find Sam and his team. He was obviously right all along. I *have* lost my focus. Perhaps we can still help. Erase the green board and delete all the video surveillance of our facility for the last three months. Then, get packed up. I am sure military commanders will be relieved that I will not be breathing down their necks any time soon."

Chapter 5

Nations Pride silently made its way back through the subterranean channel, re-emerging above the waterline in the belly of Joleen Teal's mysterious island. The Island's residents were lining the river's banks, anxiously awaiting a report. Only six of the ten-member team disembarked. Ms. Teal immediately rallied everyone's attention and requested a microphone: "Just so you know, our exploration was successful. However, it was not without incident. Four members of our team were left behind, our circumstances requiring a diversion to keep the United States military away from the area. Thus, I am ordering a full security cloaking of our island for the next thirty days. To quench your curiosity about our find; we have succeeded in locating the lost city of … *Atlantis*."

For a moment, all stood in the grip of silence, Joleen and her team awaiting a response. Suddenly, a wave of applause and shouting split the air with a decibel level rivaling a Seahawks touchdown at Century Link Field in Seattle. A sudden rhythmic throbbing of drumbeats ensued along with various groups breaking out in circle dances to celebrate their discovery. Joseph Hawk could not help but join in, immediately reaching into his buckskin pack and pulling out a dream web, his body moving effortlessly to the native beat while reaching high in the air with his favorite relic, capturing this moment forever in time.

The victory dances continued for at least a couple of hours, Joleen's face glowing with excitement over their accomplishments. However, she finally had to put a halt to the happy ceremony because time was not going to favor anyone's procrastination. Re-addressing her teams of advisors and giving specific instructions, the work of cloaking the island got underway.

Only two days into their work, Joleen received a message from Choctaw Nation Security, stating; "Inquiry into whereabouts of Captain Sam O'Brien, Buddy Gold, James Powell, and five others linked to the cruise ship Ocean Gem. Their apparent escort is a woman of unknown identity. A picture produced in our office in Durant, Oklahoma reveals one---Joleen Teal. We gave no response to the military officer requesting your identity, one ... Admiral George McCauley. Princess, we need to talk." The communiqué was signed, Nathan Teal.

Joleen halfway expected an inquiry ... eventually. Thinking back, she should have requested the ships surveillance cameras be turned off during the time of her visit. In all the excitement of Tooneys discovery, her aggressive nature caused her to forget that one detail. Yet, who knows, perhaps that little slip up would prove valuable. She made haste to the office of Joseph Hawk, also requesting the presence of James Powell, Charlie, and Carlynn. Having read the message, James Powell was the first to respond. Addressing Joseph, James asked; "What is the proper response to an individual who has proven himself a *fool?*"

Joseph contemplated the question for a few moments before making a reply, knowing James was referring to the Admiral: "Arrogance always results in negative consequences. No one is immune to its corrosive effect on relationships, especially ... friendships. However, never forget that everyone deserves a chance to grow, to learn from their mistakes and take comfort in others willingness to forgive." Turning to Joleen he added;

"Your papa is a wise man, a master at recognizing a forked tongue and twisted thinking. Share with him your concern and weigh his advice as to how to proceed with the Admiral."

Joleen agreed, insisting though that communication with her father be channeled through the Seminole Nation in Florida. James Powell would be accompanying her, Nations Pride escorting them to an outpost near Nassau, covertly staging their voyage to the United States mainland.

Boarding a tricked-out forty-foot-fishing boat on a small atoll was something of a tease for Joleen. She could not resist the urge to hook into a big old tuna. The skipper of the boat was certainly not going to argue, even though his instructions from Joseph Hawk were to make haste to West Palm Beach where pre-arranged transportation would be awaiting James' and Joleen's arrival. Joleen melted the skipper with a simple wink from her beautiful blue eyes, causing the man to flex his arms and chest as he got out a couple of poles and loaded up for tuna. It took only about thirty minutes before one of the reels started screaming. The pressure on the rod was unforgiving, an incredibly big fish spooling the reel. Harnessing Joleen's gear to the line of another pole the deck hand cast the spent tackle into the water. After peeling off another two hundred yards of line, the fish began to yield to the constant pressure.

It took another hour to retrieve the original pole at which time the deck hand quickly locked it in the fighting belt, shouting; *"Reel, reel, reel!"*

Another half-hour passed, Joleen's arms burning like fire, yet her determination to land this fish was continuing unabated. The five hundred pound prize finally weakened to the point of succumbing to the grueling battle, a beautiful silhouette rising to the surface and glistening in the morning light like that of a polished shield in the tight grip of a Greek warrior at Marathon. It was in that moment that the fish's defeat saddened Joleen, her previous encounter with the big cod in the beautiful cavern smothering her aggression, causing her to remember her own words about earth's creatures and this planet being a shared experience. As the massive bluefin finally glided near the boat, the deckhand reached for a harpoon in order to dispatch it. Joleen violently whacked the young man's arm with her rod and shouted, *"NO! Take the hook out and let it go! We cannot kill it!"*

James understood … but the skipper snapped back; *"Hey, I need the money from that fish! This is how I make a living!"*

Joleen stood her ground, pointing her finger at him with eyes blazing; *"I said let it go! I will pay you for value of the fish! Just, let it go!"*

The skipper backed off, mumbling to the deckhand, "Okay, do what she says." Then turning to Joleen he snarled; *"Seven thousand dollars lady;* the release of that fish just cost you seven thousand *additional dollars!* Letting it go is just *stupid!"*

James held out his arms, comforting Joleen and calming her down. It took a moment; however, bristling up she began quizzing her obnoxious young opponent: "So, this is *your* boat ... Captain?"

"Yes, this is *my* vessel."

"So, that means you *own* the boat?"

He mumbled under his breath, "Yeah, I wish."

"Whose boat is it then?"

"It is actually owned by some big corporation. Nevertheless, I am the *decision maker* when it comes to matters pertaining to its operation!"

"Just who is this big corporation you are talking about?"

"I don't know; Teal something."

"Oh, you mean ... Teal enterprises?"

"Yeah, I guess that's who it is. Why, what's it to you?"

"Nothing really; it is just that I always feel the need to acquaint myself with my employees. Oh, I am sorry, did I not introduce myself? I am Ms. Teal, CEO of Teal enterprises. I was unaware of our company's acquisition of this amazing craft. It is a beauty. By the way, your severance check will be awaiting our arrival on the mainland; that is of course, unless you suddenly feel the need to conjure up an *apology!*"

The skipper's face grew pale, his eyes shifting to James as if hoping Joleen's words were a hoax. James shrugged and offered, "She is not kidding. I suggest you take a big bite of humble pie and follow her suggestion. Believe me, mister, this is a woman you do not want to tick-off."

The skipper sighed, slowly re-engaging eye contact with Joleen: "Sorry … Ms. Teal. I get a bit testy when it comes to catching a big fish and … then having to release it. I, uh, hope you understand."

"I do understand, Skipper. It is probably along the lines of how I feel when someone calls me *stupid!*"

The man hung his head, tightly closing his eyes, cringing from the realization that his knee-jerk response to the woman's request just put his employment in jeopardy. After a quiet moment he slowly raised his head; "Ms. Teal, I really am sorry. Please allow me to remain on your staff. What just happened … will not happen again."

Joleen did not hesitate with her reply; "Apology accepted. Now, we need to make a beeline to West Palm Beach. When we arrive, you and your deckhand are to prepare this vessel for our return and only accept communications from either Mr. Powell or myself. What we are doing should not take long."

Chapter 6

Captain O'Brien's history lesson was met with hushed silence, the captives paying attention to every detail. All of them were survivors of historically strange and unexpected events periodically gripping the Bermuda Triangle, the cause remaining unexplainable even to seasoned scientists. The most difficult part for the survivors came when Sam took a stick and scribbled a graph in the sand revealing just how much time had passed since their disappearances. For some it was decades or centuries: for Malanai, millenniums. She was one of the residents of ancient Atlantis who managed to survive the cataclysmic effect of an asteroid colliding with the Earth. The captives' faces began taking on frowns of despair. Buddy Gold then took over the conversation, explaining the rise and fall of kingdoms and various forms of government that men contrived in hopes of providing the ultimate panacea for the world's populace. The sad reality was that all had failed, in spite of the valiant efforts of well meaning individuals. However, events of the past few decades caused most of history to pale into insignificance. The world today is suffering from a spiritual pandemic due in part to the hotbed of sex scandals rocking Christendom, as well as the carrying out of horrific crimes of terror in lands around the world by various factions of Islam. Buddy concluded; "And somehow religious leaders continue to have the people, including world rulers, duped into thinking that their influence is crucial for their respective nation's survival even though the actions of the clergy have spawned the divisions that are at the root of each nation's problems. It is no wonder that a growing segment of the world's population has had enough of the hypocrisy." Then looking over at Ben and Malanai he added, "From your description of what you just went through, it sounds like the same sickening dread was rocking your world too."

Ben nodded and replied; "It took us awhile, but we finally got the chance to break our captors yoke and escape. I do agree with your assessment of the root cause of the problem. The crazed cleric in charge of our captivity was obsessed with power." Looking around, Ben smiled at his friends and chided; "Aside from his arrogance, the man stunk to high heaven. It is a wonder that his head did not rot off from never changing that ridiculous head wrap."

Laughter ensued as each one pitched in, making jokes about the head wrap, Anders quipping, "It was to his advantage there are no flies here. They would have gnawed his scalp off a long time ago."

After catching his breath from laughing so hard, Ben continued; 'What amazes me though is; how did the *fish* know? They were the ones starting the event leading to our escape, and during the battle, it was obvious, at least to me, that their target was our oppressors. A big swordfish scooped up a spear and charged right down the throat of a croc, saving my life. He then reemerged out of the throat of the beast, gave me a wink, and continued to fight. The plesiosaurs were also fighting for us, picking off the pterodactyls that came swooping in low for a kill. Then to top it off, dolphins came out of seemingly nowhere, speeding our group to a place of safety and transporting us through a breach in our prison web. Where did they all come from? Most of these creatures are not residents of these waters."

Sam, Chloe, Buddy, and Tooney listened intently to Ben's review. Coupled with their own experience, none of what Ben recounted surprised them in the least. It was Ben's next statement that floored Sam; "The big cod, that *big cod*, he seems to be the leader. I watched him while the dolphins were helping us through the breach in the web and I swear he was the one staging our escape. I am telling you; there is something amazing and special about that fish."

Sam smiled, replying to Ben, "We agree. I think now is a good time to fill you in on more details of our expedition. We are convinced that that fish and his companions are somehow trying to help us unlock the mystery surrounding this network of caverns."

Conversation ensued for quite some time, Sam taking the lead in explaining their expedition, discoveries, and Tooney's special connection with the young dolphin. Everyone listened intently, their faces glowing with excitement over the progress Sam and his team were making in piecing together an ancient puzzle. Wrapping it up, Sam concluded; "This is the adventure of all adventures people, and you are in it. What do you say we do some exploring?"

The magnificent bay and the surrounding area reminded Sam of Joleen Teal on the day she first arrived at Cape Hatteras' shipyard, her stunning beauty capturing the very soul of a sailor's life. He smiled when thinking of what Joleen would do if she were in the spot he was in, knowing she was probably thinking the same thing about him. The bottom line; 'let's get to work'. Sam put one hand on Ben's shoulder and, pointing off in the distance with his other hand, asked; "Is there any way to scale those cliffs behind the waterfall?"

Ben's reply; "No, there is not. We already searched it out and there is no passage. We are just grateful that we have enough living area to re-group and an abundance of food to provide for our needs."

Sam stood in silence for a few moments, his mind racing with ideas about the remaining caverns and the possibility of additional pockets of dark matter, which could prove useful for their return to Joleen Teal's island. He had an idea, asking Ben for an audience with Malanai. Ben found her gathering berries along the edge of a meandering creek. Sneaking up behind her, he whisked her off her feet and spun her in a circle before turning her around and tenderly kissing her. For a long time she had been his beacon of hope, always encouraging him to look to the future instead of pining away in uncertain circumstances. She agreed to speak with Sam.

Walking hand-in-hand and sharing some of the deliciously sweet fruit, they approached Sam who was knee deep in water, being intrigued by the variety of sea life lining the shallows of the bay. Seeing Ben and Malanai's watery silhouettes in his peripheral vision, Sam turned, quickly reaching his hand out to greet Malanai. When she looked up, he gasped; the woman's eyes were glowing translucent green, like sparkling emeralds surrounded by a golden band of seven glistening triangles pointing inward toward the pupil. Before Sam could utter a word, Ben grabbed hold of his arm, leaning forward and whispering, "That was my first reaction. It's okay; she is used to it."

Malanai sensed Sam's embarrassment and offered, "Please, come over to the shore and have some fruit; I just now gathered it."

Sam was definitely feeling ill at ease, trying hard not to glare at the woman's entrancing eyes, and apologizing: "I am so sorry Malanai, please forgive me."

Ben grasped Malanai's hand, the two chuckling for a moment and Ben replying, "It is okay Captain. At least your response didn't cause you to slide off a rock and plunge into the water like I did." Malanai chuckled even harder, cupping her face in her hands. Ben then asked Sam, "So what are we going to discuss?"

"I was wondering if Malanai has any ideas of how we can get to any of the caverns surrounding this area, seeing that we cannot traverse any of the cliffs surrounding our present location."

Malanai nodded her head. She then spoke in an unusually sad tone; "A long time ago I also had a companion, much like the creature the little boy rides, the web in the back of the bay specifically designed for keeping him away. My evil Uncle was punishing me for trying to use my friend in an attempt to help his slaves escape."

Ben looked dumbfounded; "So, the guy in the head wrap was … *your uncle?*"

Tearing up Malanai said, "I should have told you. I am so sorry. I did not want to put you in any further danger. I was afraid that if you found out … you would not want me."

"Not want you? Oh, Malanai, there is nothing anyone could do to cause me not to want you; I love you."

Wrapping her in his arms, Ben took a moment to let the emotion pass. Sam backed away, waiting for Malanai to be consoled before questioning her regarding her friend. Ben took her for a little walk, gently reassuring her of his devotion. Meanwhile, Sam rounded up Buddy, Chloe, and Tooney, hoping that whatever Malanai had to share about her friend could give them some ideas.

Returning with Malanai after a brief stroll through the tropical forest, Ben's eyes were as big as saucers. "Captain," he said, "you had better be ready for a wild ride because, if Malanai is successful in finding the friend she just told me about, you are going to think you are in a cartoon." Turning to Malanai Ben nodded and said, "It is okay, you can call him now."

After swimming out a short distance Malanai submerged, opening her mouth under water and blaring out a deafening shriek, the intensity paralyzing every creature in the bay. The audible even affected the water's surface, causing it to quiver as though a tingling were rolling up its spine. All those gathered at the water's edge felt the piercing grip of the frequency's energy, impairing their ability to so much as twitch. Then, re-emerging, Malanai waited patiently for a reply, casually staying afloat, motioning Ben and the others to join her in the water. Tooney waded out and started beating his hands on the surface to call for Schooner, the terrified little dolphin responding immediately. Tooney grabbed on to the dolphin's dorsal fin and the two began frolicking around, Malanai joining them, skillfully mimicking Schooner's porpoising in and out of the water. Socrates and his friends, including the plesiosaurs, moved in closer to shore, wondering what was going on. The rest of the humans also responded to Malanai's invitation and began wading out into the water. Sam and Buddy strapped on their dive masks to check out what was happening beneath the surface. It took only a moment before Socrates and Poker were face to face with the men, staring at each other with a heightened sense of connection. Sam calmly raised his head out of the water, motioning for Ben to join him and Buddy. Ben moved slowly, and after catching up asked, "What?" Sam pointed towards Socrates and Poker, causing Ben to smile, his mind once again surging with excitement over the strange bond he was feeling with the big cod and swordfish. Ben felt an urge to reach out his hand for a response from the fish. Socrates asked Poker, "What do you think?"

Poker replied, "Well, I wouldn't pull it … if that's what you mean."

Socrates rolled his eyes; "You really are a doofus." He then brushed Ben's outreached hand with his fin, and backed away. The surreal moment was enough validation for Sam's conjecture that somehow, these two fish, along with their companions, were part of unraveling an ancient mystery. The challenge now was … coordinating their effort.

Chapter 7

The merriment in the water continued for some time. Everyone was playing games, Peetie being heard crying out for Kaimana to '*stop it*'. The mischievous plesiosaur was swimming under the little rockfish, raising him up and flinging him backwards, leaving Peetie crashing hard back into the water. NuiMalu had to break it up for fear of Peetie getting hurt. Of course Kaimana always had an excuse; "Aw dad, my brother just missed catching him. It really is a fun game."

Peetie replied, "Yeah, well, just wait till we get out of here! I will introduce you to my friend Jake and we will see who goes flying through the air!"

Kaimana just shrugged off the comment and took off to play with his sister and friends. Only moments after disappearing he came storming back. Sam's eyes opened wide, an immense wave building up in the bay and heading their way. Scrambling to get everyone out of the water and to the safety of higher ground, he shouted to Malanai, *"What is it?"* She did not answer, turning instead into the swell and disappearing. Ben was panicking, not knowing what to expect, and feeling his life would be shattered if anything bad happened to Malanai. Socrates and his friends began scattering, seeking immediate shelter from an immense wall of silt-laden water billowing up and rapidly engulfing every square inch of the pristine bay in its frightening wake. Ben began screaming, *"Malanai, Malanai,"* when instantly the bay exploded from the emergence of at least a thousand magnificent sea horses, each some 10 to 12 feet in height, charging in a thunderous romp, resembling a herd of wild mustangs across the high desert ranges of Arizona. Approaching the shallows with heads held high and proud, they began forming a wide circle, positioning themselves like attendants in a royal court. The bay then took on a deafening silence, the water settling and the herd now motionless. A moment later the area in the middle of the circle began boiling and swirling before violently erupting from the emergence of a great, 15 foot stallion, his massive webbed fins spreading wide like the wings of a dragon, lifting Malanai high in the air, her arms in a tight grip around his head, his snout supporting her torso. The steed's eyes were a kaleidoscope of patterns and color, changing with every movement, the flow of generated energy shooting sparks across his jet-black pupils. The golden bands of glistening triangles in Malanai's eyes began glowing like electrum, a field of energy building up in their emerald core, growing stronger and stronger until suddenly … a paralyzing flash of light resembling a bolt of lightning ignited between them, the fiery conduit locking them in its grip, restoring ages of memories past. Malanai then swung around on the magnificent stallions back as he reared high and began proudly cantering around within the circle of the herd.

Witnessing the fairytale reunion, Ben and the others stood speechless. They watched as Malanai masterfully handled her mount, a royal display of equine mastery, the spirited steed basking in the moment of rekindling a friendship he sorely missed. Together they used to entertain the inhabitants of Atlantis with unique performances that intimidated even the greatest of warriors. There was not another creature in the ocean that rivaled Malanai's beloved---Revelator. She named him for his unique ability to memorize every canyon, cavern, bay, passage, and trench in the ocean. Together they would disappear for long periods, riding the ocean currents in search of adventure. Malanai was so happy to have Rev back, her face glowing with excitement.

Socrates and his friends watched in amazement, the stallion cocking his head in triumph. Jazzy and Baaya could not help themselves, the little angelfish busting out in song, the young tiger shark moving to the lyrics:

"Riding high, across a pristine sea
Spirits high, this is where we want to be
Romping around, just my friends and me
Waiting for no one, just living a life that's free.
    Yeah, we take it to the limit when we feel the need to dance
    Yes we take it to the limit every time we get the chance
    Rocking in the current and swaying to our song
    Giving no thought to stopping … dancing all day long.
So join with us in grooving across this great big sea
And dance like you mean it, like there's no place else to be
Come romp around with friends like Jazzy and me
And give your life a lift … because you really are free.
    Yeah, take it to the limit when you feel the need to dance
    Yes, take it to the limit every time you get the chance
    Rock with us in the current and feel the power of our song
    And give no thought to stopping … Do it all day long
    Yeah, give no thought to stopping … Do it all --- day --- long."

Catching sight of Jazzy, being amused by her rhythmic movements, one of the mares submerged, and began mimicking the dance. Suddenly all the seahorses joined in, leaving Rev and Malanai perplexed, the stallion feeling someone was stealing his moment of glory. Malanai burst into laughter after submerging and seeing the little angelfish and young tiger shark leading the seahorses in song and dance. She motioned for Ben and the others to join her and see what was going on. Tooney ran into waste deep water and started pounding his hands flat on the surface, Schooner responding in an instant, the duo excitedly hurrying to join the excitement.

Chloe's instincts began sweeping her away, quickly swimming right up to one of the mares, surprising it at first, but then gently wrapping her arms around its head. Staring the creature in the eyes she waited, and … nothing. Malanai dismounted and swam over to her: "If you are waiting for sparks, it is not going to happen. She is not resisting which means you have already connected with her. Go ahead, mount up, and ride. Chloe quickly rolled onto the back of the mare, gently motioning her forward. Malanai remounted Rev and the two led Chloe and the mare out into the bay with Tooney and Schooner tagging along. Sam and Buddy ran back to the shore, grabbing their dive masks and swimming into deeper water to catch a glimpse of what was going on beneath the surface. Sam could not believe his eyes. The same little angelfish from the canyon, along with the dancing tiger shark were performing in the middle of the seahorses, a large group of mares following the smaller fishes lead. Sam actually started moving to the aquatic gyrations. Tapping Sam on the shoulder and motioning him back to the surface, Buddy removed his mask, quipping; "Uh, I don't know about you pal, but I am thinking; it must have been something we ate or drank. This is nuts."

Sam smiled and replied, "Well, at least it is fun. I really think Malanai and that stallion are going to be able to help us. C'mon, let's join the others and play a while. I have my eyes on one of those mares over there. I hope she doesn't whack the daylights out of me when I put my arms around her head."

Buddy chuckled; "Just a suggestion; I would remove the mask. It makes you look … well, um, challenged."

The activity in the water continued for quite a long time, each of the forty-three captives following Malanai's direction and bonding with their chosen mounts. With spirits soaring, all were responding with a heightened sense of purpose. Sam was also successful in his selection of the mare he had his eyes on earlier, while Buddy picked out a large and powerful young stallion with fearless countenance.

Socrates was feeling a bit perplexed about how the appearance of the seahorses would affect he and his friends. He approached NuiMalu and Mau: "So, what do you think is going on?"

Mau replied, "Give me a moment; I'll find out."

Mau sped forward to the front of the herd, breaching high out of the water in front of Rev, the stallion rearing up, snorting his defiance of the intruder. Sensing a confrontation, Malanai jumped off Rev, grabbing on to Chloe's mount and motioning the others to retreat. Sizing one another up, the great plesiosaur and mighty stallion submerged. Underwater the two began laughing, Rev stating, "You old dinosaur; you still splashing around?"

"Yeah, well look at you; what is up with the grand entry into the bay? You seahorses certainly have a flare for the dramatic. However, before you go romping off into who knows where, you need to know about that group of fish you are leaving behind in the bay. They are the ones who rescued your rider and all of her friends. So, I think you need to dial your royal presence down a notch, because when you hear what they have been through, well, you can believe me; you are going to want to be in on this adventure."

Respecting Mau's words of caution and staring back into the bay, Rev nodded and replied, "Let them know we will be back in a little while. I need some time with my rider. I have missed her so much."

Mau and Rev then slapped fins, retreating to their groups. Malanai remounted Rev who once again reared high before prancing away with his entire herd in tow. Mau lazily made his way back into the shallows where the other fish were waiting with NuiMalu and his family. Socrates was confused, shrugging and asking, "So, what happened?"

Mau stretched his fins out wide, flexing while resuming position; "Someone has to keep that old hoss in line." He then gave Nui a wink and a smile, his son remembering his dad's stories of the stallion and how close of a friendship they enjoyed when they were young. In response to Socrates, Mau assured him, "The herd will be back in a little while. However, I am thinking that a little hospitality, perhaps like … sharing a meal, would be an appropriate gesture upon their return." Looking over at Poker he asked, "What do you think? You could arrange for that, right?"

Poker responded, "Oh, ho, ho, yeah; a seahorse tail straightening party would be a real nice touch." He then took off, rounding up his friends to help prepare the mischievous feast.

Chapter 8

Joleen Teal and her cousin James arrived at the Big Cypress Seminole Reservation just after sundown. The village was very quiet, the only business remaining open being a small café located at the edge of a swamp close to the AH-TAH-THI-KI Museum. After walking in and looking around Joleen began choking up, her thoughts retreating to a time when life was oh so simple. The waitress smiled, and without a word began escorting James and Joleen to a rear corner table overlooking the water, its glassy surface capturing the magnificence of the first sliver of a new moon beginning its mute accent across the sky. There to greet them was an extremely handsome man with long graying hair pulled back into a ponytail, his forehead graced with a wide, beaded turquoise headband. His eyes filled with tears as his daughter lunged into his arms, clutching him tightly and sobbing; "Oh daddy, I have missed you so much. Please forgive me for staying away so long."

"My little princess, I have been comforted by the fact that you are making real changes in this world. Believe me, your mom and I thrive on the pride we feel over your accomplishments."

James gave them a moment before saying, "Hello Uncle Nate. It's been a long time."

Nathan Teal was surprised, only now realizing that it was his nephew James Powell accompanying Joleen. While still holding his daughter in his arms Nathan said, "It is good to see you nephew. You have been keeping an eye on my princess, have you?"

"Yes Uncle; strange circumstances have reunited us and I am committed to helping her."

Nathan responded, "Your integrity and the path you have chosen in life bring great pride to our family James. Remember what your uncles and I used to call you when you were young?"

James lowered his head and smiled, "Yes, I remember."

"Far-Reach; we called you Far-Reach, because we could see something special about you, your inner spirit always soaring with a desire for adventure. I am so happy to know that you and my daughter's paths have crossed once again. Now, let us sit and enjoy some food. I called early to have them prepare a special meal. It was always Joleen's favorite and, if I remember correctly, you also shared a love for it when you would come to visit."

Joleen and James were thrilled to sit down to the tantalizing aroma of crawfish jambalaya. The server brought out huge bowls filled with the delectable little crustaceans mixed in with rice, andouille sausage, and a variety of veggies and southern spices. Complimenting the main course was a large square slab of steaming hot cornbread sided with fresh creamery butter and prickly-pear syrup lightly tainted with cinnamon. The dessert course proved equally impressive; a deep pan sugar latticed blackberry cobbler topped off with a scoop of homemade vanilla ice cream, the addictive combination of sweet and tart flavors making their jaws ache, yet forcing their palates into craving more. All that, coupled with large glasses of sweet sun tea laced with fresh mint leaves, blissfully completed a meal that kings of the earth would die for. Not a word was uttered until their palates were completely satisfied, Joleen breaking the silence with an embarrassing muffled belch, wiping her mouth and quickly apologizing; "What can I say; it even sounds good."

James and Nathan broke into laughter, the comical moment igniting memories of a simpler life on the reservation. After paying the tab, Nathan offered, "We need some sleep so that our minds will be fresh in the morning. Come with me, I have arranged accommodations at the house of an old friend."

Joleen, as usual, was ready to start their conversation about what was happening on her island immediately. However, James replied to his uncle; "It is a good plan. We need to be thinking clearly when we share with you what has been going on."

Joleen acquiesced to her cousins' decision, stating; "I suppose some rest couldn't hurt. James, if you don't mind, I will ride with my dad and you can follow in the rental car."

The following morning revealed the comforting pace of a sleepy village, as peaceful a setting as any either James or Joleen could ever remember on the mainland. Nathan sought out a shady knoll by the water's edge, bringing with him a thermos of coffee, some hot fritters, and a blanket to sit on. Once they were all comfortable Nathan inquired, "So my Princess, why would a Navy Admiral be seeking your whereabouts? Tell me, what have you been up to?"

Joleen and James spent several hours discussing how their adventure got started and what had transpired since. Nathan never flinched or uttered a word. He just sat on the edge of the blanket scribing picture notes in a clump of dried mud with a stick. Joleen finally wrapped up the review with her head slumping in her hands and stating, "I should have *erased* the video of those last few days at the shipyard. It was a *stupid mistake!*"

Nathan took his daughter's hand, tenderly kissed it, and said, "My Princess; you made a judgment call based on something that could negatively affect the whole of humanity. When an individual's heart is set afire with such a discovery, one's mind cannot preclude all the variables involved in keeping it confidential. From what you have shared with me, you and your friends have done the right thing by testing the theory first. Now, regarding the Admiral, I will return to Durant in the morning to assess his story and what it is he wants. I will be in touch shortly. You two need to return to the island and focus on your rescue plan. I am sure Captain O'Brien is as anxious as you are for what comes next."

Joleen hugged her dad tightly, his encouragement firing up her spirit. She had just one more thing to say; "Daddy, once you meet with the Admiral, I would like to arrange for you and mama to come to the island. Please daddy, we need you there. Joseph Hawk is a sage and competent advisor, but he has his hands full. I would feel a lot more comfortable with you and mom helping him with oversight."

Caressing Joleen's face in his hands Nathan replied, "I thought you would never ask. I am getting tired of wasting so much time preparing to relive the past every year. As a people we Choctaws, as well as the other indigenous tribes of this land, got the shaft; okay. Well, actually, not okay; but that is history now and nothing can change it. Remembering history is one thing; reliving tragedy only stokes the anger of a new generation, flooding the heart with negative emotions. We need to move on and get over it. My precious daughter, reports of your vision and the work you are doing on your island is igniting a true beacon of hope for all our tribes as well as anyone desiring a peaceful existence with their fellow man. We are so proud of you. I will speak with your mother. I am sure your invitation will excite her."

After hugging her father one last time, Joleen followed James to their car and the two set off, back to West Palm Beach.

The young skipper of the fishing vessel was keeping busy while awaiting his employer's arrival, having prepared an array of fresh fruit and light sandwiches for the voyage back to the outpost near Nassau. Joleen could not help but engage him in conversation; "Well, Skipper, I am delighted to see you so prompt and ready to go. This is what I call service."

His reply; "Yes maam, we are fueled up and ready to depart. Any last requests before we pull away?"

"I have only one request young man. Would you mind running over to the fish market before we leave? I would like a fresh filet of blue fin tuna. Oh, and uh, make sure it is … sashimi grade."

The skippers jaw dropped, his eyes just about popping out of his head, James and the deck hand instantly busting a gut at the man's reaction to his employer's satirical request. Joleen quipped, "Lighten up Captain, it's just a tinge of Choctaw humor. And by the way, if you feel a sudden need to change your trousers, I suggest you do it before we pull away from the dock."

The skipper reacted by rolling his eyes; "Real funny Ms. Teal, that was real funny. You do standup, do you?"

Joleen welcomed the return, suddenly taking a liking to the young Captain, acknowledging his humble response to remain in her employ, yet brave enough to engage her sly comment. He then called for the deckhand to cast off the dock lines, and they began their trek back to the outpost.

Chapter 9

Disembarking the fishing vessel in the dark on a small atoll made Joleen feel a bit nervous, thinking military satellites were probably monitoring the area. She and James waited for the fishing vessel's lights to disappear into the distance before signaling Nations Pride for their pick up. Once onboard, Corey Coulson hurried them into the Raptor's control room. Charlie was busy tracking satellite images. Joleen responded in a tone of shock: *"Charlie ...* what in the world---are you downloading data from military satellites?"

"Yep; two can play this game. I completed this program this morning. I was working on it earlier on the island while we were preparing the Raptor. What is cool is that I can actually *upload* information into the satellites databanks to erase what we do not want them to see. It is like the billions of images your brain processes through your eyes every second.

Memory banks work on things important, filtering out the peripheral images that are not important."

James asked, "What is going on for you to have to do that?"

"Well, Joleen left orders to track satellites and we have detected a heightened activity in this area. So, Corey and I decided to use our ship to implement the new program, testing its capacity to mess with the military's orbiting probes. Actually, it has been fun. Here, look at this; we recorded it just before noon. See that pile of floating debris; well, we were able to upload a link to a satellite to make it look like a two hundred foot octopod. Now, watch the reaction."

Coming up on the screen were six helicopters launched from an aircraft carrier. Charlie was even able to pick up their audio, the pilots being heard arguing with the ship's commander that it was a simple debris field and not a 'Kraken'.

Joleen started chuckling, responding with a single word, "*Charlie!*"

Shrugging his shoulders Charlie replied, "Hey, it gets boring just waiting around. We had to keep busy doing something constructive."

With one hand stroking his chin James offered, "I suppose it can't hurt. At least we are confusing the ones we need to keep off our backs."

Joleen thought about Charlie's actions for but a moment, quietly leaving the control room shaking her head.

Back on the island, Joseph Hawk was nervously pacing back and forth while awaiting Joleen's arrival. Once the dock lines were draped over the mooring links, Joleen and her crew were hurried away to the war room. The facility was set up to respond to any danger affecting the island and its residents. Joseph and Carlynn, as well as a team of graphic artists, took downloaded images provided earlier by Charlie and created a three dimensional map of their previous journey to the caverns. Using Joleen's speculation of a two and a half mile radius from cavern to cavern and triangulating from the center of the canyon, they used the distance to and between the first two caverns as their starting point. Next, they plotted a mock-up for the balance of the caverns entries using the exact same distance between caverns as their guide for the overall diameter of the ancient city. Charlie was the first to identify the symmetry: "Oh man, this is crazy. Do you see it?"

"See what?" Carlynn replied.

Charlie asked Joseph; "Can you stack the image of the caverns with a holographic compass? Make the northernmost cavern top dead center, zero degrees."

Pondering the request for but a moment, his wife's face took on a look of wonder, mumbling; "Could it be?"

Focusing on the compass settings surrounding the graphic of the caverns, Carlynn smiled, turning to her husband and hugging him. It took Joleen and Joseph a moment, but they too finally caught on, responding without a word, gazing in quiet repose. Charlie was heard whispering, "twenty three point four five degrees; the angle of earth's tilt on its axis. How did they know ---? If this is accurate, it is the perfect calculation for urban design. Building cities today with this kind of ecliptic symmetry could result in stymieing social problems caused by population density while literally eliminating the need for growth boundaries. It also appears obvious why the builders set the crystal in the canyon; the location offered the perfect nucleus for streaming light through their municipal network of caverns, a way of capturing the magnificence of their creation during a solar event without any obstruction."

Joseph Hawk, with arms folded and locked across his chest, nodded several times, being impressed by the ancients' incredible knowledge of architecture. Yet, he had something to add to the puzzle; "While you were gone, some of our team began wondering about the possibility of re-fitting our Raptor with the capacity of the existing laser in addition to a modified version of the original---just in case?"

Charlie thought for a moment; "Well, what are the chances of acquiring another rough diamond big enough to cut to the size of the one we are using?"

Joseph smiled, motioning to two of his staff who quickly exited the room. The young women returned about fifteen minutes later, directing a fork lift driver to a specific loading area before signaling him to lower a very large wooden crate. Puzzled, Charlie looked at the container, then at Joseph; "So, what have we here?"

Joseph reached for a key in his pocket and proceeded to unlock two large padlocks hanging from work-hardened steel hasps securing the crate's door shut. Swinging the door open, he reached inside and gripped a large handle, pulling out a secondary container which was supported on a four wheel dolly. Charlie snorted a comical chuckle, "What in the world---?"

Joseph offered; "It was your request my friend, so you get to open it. Go ahead, pop the latches and lift the lid. It is hinged so you don't have to worry about it falling off."

Inside the enormous box, sitting on a padded display, was the largest uncut diamond Charlie had ever seen, being at least three times the original size of the one he was currently using for the raptor's laser. For a moment, Charlie could hardly breathe, finally turning to Joseph and asking, "Where did you manage to find this?"

Joseph's reply; "We have our sources. Now, can you refit the Raptor?"

Charlie's thoughts were exploding with possibilities, a huge smile slowly spreading across his face; "Yes, I believe I can. Please get this to the stonecutter's lab. Also, move the Raptor back into the new technologies warehouse. I have a very cool idea."

Chapter 10

Nathan Teal identified himself to the Admiral only by his first and middle names, along with his official tribal title: Nate Batiste, Commissioner of Inner Tribal Police. George McCauley's belligerence left Nathan unimpressed, the man having a streak of arrogance a mile long. His demonstrative demand for an audience with Joleen Teal was only resulting in a response of cold silence from Nathan, the Admiral acting as though the Choctaw Nation was at his bid and call: *"What do you not understand,"* he barked; *"I need to see her now!"*

That was when his young Lieutenant, Randy Christopher, held up his hand, trying to quell the Admiral's frustration at Nathan's lack of a reply. Interrupting, Randy responded, "Mr. Batiste, I am so sorry. If you and the Admiral do not mind"---the Lieutenant glanced at the Admiral, giving him a visual signal to take a seat and calm down, the Admiral responding with a scowl on his face. The young man continued; "Please, Commissioner, let me fill you in on what has happened over the past few months."

Extending his hand, Nathan motioned for the young man to proceed. The Lieutenant was calm and proficient with his explanation of events from the time of Sam O'Brien's first call to the Admiral's office right up until the present moment. He concluded, "Please, Sir, we really do want to help." Then, looking the Admiral in the eye, he concluded; "My boss is a good man. However, he has a serious problem with … *diplomacy!*"

The Admiral's challenging glare caused Randy to add, "See: case closed."

Nathan finally broke into a grin, yet taking a moment to collect his thoughts before replying: "You men must know … the Choctaw Nation is a sovereign entity, and history does not favor our responding kindly to those making demands of us. We are the indigenous peoples of this land. Therefore, I suggest you temper any request with dignity and respect. You will remain as our guests for the next few days. Tomorrow I will introduce you to our tribal leaders who will educate you in the progress of our people. During this time, you will refrain from any further mention of the name Joleen

Teal. As you well know Admiral, some inquiries are best kept confidential. I have arranged for your stay at one of our lodges down by the river under the guise of discussing the history of our World War 1 code talkers. Please accept our hospitality."

The Admiral responded to Nathan's outstretched hand with a tinge of reluctance, the man's unpretentious, yet firm demeanor catching him off guard. Lieutenant Christopher got up from his chair, politely bowing in Southern custom before shaking Nathan's hand. Nathan was impressed with this discerning young man and his unique ability to steer the course of a conversation away from confrontation. Nathan then offered, "Come with me. We are starting an end of harvest Pow-Wow today and I am sure you will be pleased with the food and entertainment. Addressing the young Lieutenant he asked, "You play stickball?"

"I played Lacrosse in college."

"Close enough; you can join in the games."

Chapter 11

Only two days after Joleen's return to her island, strobe lights coupled with strong vibrations awakened everyone at two o'clock in the morning. The covert alarm was a sure signal their security was in danger of compromise. Joleen quickly sprinted from her lodge to a nearby staircase to board a tram, overriding its governed speed and heading straight for the Islands security office. Upon arrival she found James and Joseph already taking charge and alerting all personnel to their assigned emergency stations, this not being a drill. She asked in a panic; *"what is going on?"*

His reply; "Look at the monitor. There are two U.S. warships and a trident sub circling our perimeter."

"What could they possibly want?"

"I have no idea, but we have to be careful not to over-react. There is no indication their scanners have picked up anything unusual. We have shut down all external communications including satellite links. If we keep quiet maybe they will leave." He then requested; "Quick, Joleen, I need you to find Corey."

Corey was located---where else; sleeping at the helm aboard Nations Pride. Joleen hustled him to the security office. Seeing him enter the room James called out, "Quick, Corey, over here. What do you think; can we divert their attention?"

Corey's eyes opened wide, the sub closing in on the entrance to their subterranean canal, Nations Pride's only way out to the open ocean. Bolting for the door Corey blurted out, "We have to go *now* Sir!"

Quickly taking hold of Joleen's hand, James followed, calling out to Joseph, "maintain silence and get Charlie to speed it up on refitting the raptor!"

Within moments, Nations Pride was easing her way through the subterranean channel, Corey hoping beyond hope, they would not collide with the sub. To his favor, the island had an abrupt drop off of one thousand feet just outside the channel, allowing Nations Pride an almost vertical dive within a hundred feet of the island's visible perimeter. Under full cloaking, Corey leveled off at five hundred feet, circling underneath the belly of the submarine, the nuclear vessel not detecting their presence. Joleen and James were racking their brains as to what to do next. Corey honed in on the sub's communications, the commanders of each vessel coordinating a sweep of the entire island.

Joleen asked; "What are they looking for?"

Corey started snickering; "More than likely, Seal Team six."

Joleen smacked him on the arm, his humor a bit inappropriate at the moment. Nevertheless, Corey suddenly got an idea. While easing Nations Pride into shallower water and closer to the sub, he handed James a small list of instructions, a doodle sheet Charlie previously drew up when writing his new satellite program. James caught on immediately, instructing Corey to get two miles separation from the sub and bring Nations Pride to within six fathoms of the surface. Then taking Joleen by the hand the two hustled into the raptors control room. With eyes tightly squinted while scanning the virtual screen, he whispered; "Now, what can we target?"

Picking up the flight of a small plane about twenty miles away, just south and east of their location, he got an idea. Copying Charlie's strategy of uploading bogus imagery into a military satellite, an extremely large, strangely shaped UFO appeared out of nowhere in International air space. Both ships and the sub responded instantly, turning off course on a vector to intercept. Of course, the phantom aircraft was too fast for the ships, the circumstance demanding the assistance of the air force. Four F16s were airborne in a matter of seconds. Corey then intercepted the military's communication, the flight commander getting into an argument with the naval commanders. That is when James really laid it on, uploading a phrase from a childhood memory through an audible link to the satellite: "Ho ba de michi da? Ho da bricki mong?"

The military commanders were going crazy trying to understand the transmission. When the air squadron arrived at the coordinates given them, a twin engine Beachcraft was all they saw. Hailing its pilot, the squadron leader determined there was nothing amiss for a famous golfer being on his way to a tournament. Yet the commanders of the destroyers were still swearing that the images they were getting were those of an interstellar warship of some kind. All of a sudden, the voice of a young sailor interrupted the com, asking his Commander for permission to speak. Corey cranked up the volume: "I can decipher the code sir! The code is right here in this little book."

"*What book?* The navy does not print books full of gibberish! So, once again, *what book?*"

"My, uh, Star Trek code book Sir. I have identified the language as being … Clingon."

Laughter exploded from the helm of the ship, the Commander ready to knock the young man's head off his shoulders. However, he felt compelled to ask for the translation.

The young man took a notepad, writing out the message, decoding it with the aid of his 'official book'. "I am pretty sure it says: 'What are you looking at? You never saw a Clingon vessel before?'"

Once again, the crew at the helm busted into laughter, the Commander thanking his young crewmember for being so familiar with alien lingo. He then hailed the other vessels, calling them off, the military satellite database obviously compromised. The Flight Leader of the F16s got in a final spoof: "Air assist returning to base, Sir. Let me know if the, uh, Enterprise requires deployment."

Corey, James, and Joleen waited patiently to see if there would be any repercussions from the military, knowing the seriousness of a compromised communications link. Corey gently steered Nations Pride away from the sub and headed south, getting about fifty miles separation from the military vessels. Joleen appeared more nervous than either James or Corey had ever seen her. However, the look on her face suddenly turned fierce as she slammed her fist down on the counter surrounding the helm, threatening: "If the military wants to mess with our research, then all bets are off! We will give them more than they bargained for! Corey, get us another one hundred miles separation further south. Then pick out the closest atoll and upload another image to the next military satellite passing over. This time make it resemble a Russian destroyer. When the military closes in within twenty miles, swing us around to the east and make a loop back to home base."

James looked puzzled, "Cousin, what are you thinking?"

"There is no way the military or anyone else is going to interrupt our discovery operations! The first thing we are going to do when we get back is to find out who is responsible for targeting our island! Next, our Raptor is going to do a little stirring up of its own, even if it means shrinking the size of military fleets, if you know what I mean!"

James grabbed his cousins hand; "Joleen, you cannot incite a military conflict!"

"I will stand my ground! What price do you think they are willing to pay?"

Corey's eyes opened wide, his lips tightly closed, silently proceeding with Ms. Teal's instruction. James simply leaned back on the console with his head lowered, wondering what was going to happen next. Seething with anger, Joleen began taking on the countenance of a chieftain preparing for a last stand, adding, "We have a hostile situation on our hands gentlemen and we will *not back down!* We have discovered what we think is the heartbeat of our planet and there is no way I am going to yield our find to those who will exploit it for selfish purpose! On this day our fight begins; we will *Battle for Atlantis!"*

Chapter 12

Socrates and his friends were laughing themselves into near unconsciousness, Poker having catered the perfect feast for Rev and his returning herd. Only moments after the seahorses began gorging themselves on the vast amount of shrimp laden kelp, the bay began erupting like the vent of gas from a giant volcano. The seahorses were lurching from the uncontrollable expulsions, their tails wrapping in a reverse curl every time they 'let one go'. Not able to control the surges upsetting their digestive tracts, some were flipping awkwardly out of water, sometimes crashing back face first. It was a good thing that Malanai and the rest of the riders dismounted before the feast began. On shore, 'the Posse', the name by which the humans were collectively referring to themselves, was trying to figure out what was going on, their mounts in the bay braying in panic from obvious physical distress. After some anxious moments of sheer frustration, the seahorses retreated into deeper water. Rev was not amused over Poker's 'not so practical joke.' Racing after the herd, Mau caught up to Rev, apologizing for their mischievous prank: "I am sorry old friend; we had that joke played on us when we first arrived in the bay, and the temptation to share it with newcomers --- well, what is there to say? That was hysterical."

Rev responded, "Yeah, just great. You make my herd look like a bunch of spastic prawns and that is supposed to be funny!"

Mau was trying hard to keep from busting out laughing all over again. Rev stared him down for a moment and then started laughing himself; "You are all as funny as a mass of drifting cuda-dookey." He then looked around for a moment, edging up against Mau and whispering, "Actually, it was fun watching the mares. They are always acting so dainty. However, your friends need to be careful. Do you see that group huddling up over there? That is what our females do when they feel the urge for revenge. Tell your friends to remain vigilant, because these gals know ... payback."

Mau nodded, "Point well taken. I will make sure Poker knows that he is in for an unexpected surprise."

Rev's eyes opened wide, "Poker---did you say, *Poker*, like ... the *swordfish?*"

Appearing dumbfounded, Mau responded, "Yes---why, have you heard of him?"

"He would not happen to have a friend named ... *Socrates,* would he?"

"Yes he would. I am curious; where have you heard their names before?"

"We have been hearing more than the usual amount of whale songs lately, and the mention of two fish, a DK Cod named Socrates and a swordfish named Poker seem to be dominating the storyline. Those two are apparently ... legends."

Mau felt numb, wondering how stories of Socrates and Poker could possibly be spreading so quickly through this region. Motioning Rev away from the herd, Mau brought him back into the shallows.

Seeing their approach, Poker swallowed hard and began looking for an exit. Unable to escape his inevitable confrontation with the big stallion, it took but a second for him to revert to his usual self: Addressing Rev he asked, "You, uh, feeling better? Your herd is looking … *'EXHAUSTED'*."

Mau, once again, lost it. Rev just shook his head, looking at Mau and mumbling, "Seriously, I mean … seriously?" He then turned back to Poker who crossed his eyes and asked, "Hey, who are you two? Are you like twins … or, say … *WHAAAT?*"

This time, Rev began laughing, coughing out a choked response; "You are definitely a piece of work."

Putting his fin to his bill and appearing philosophical, Poker replied; "I could be labeled that I suppose, considering our current situation and my … in-*STINK*-tual wisdom. If you ask me, most individuals are just too serious about themselves. However, when you give them a chance to … *VENT*---well, lightens things up a bit, wouldn't you agree?"

Unbeknown to Rev, all of Socrates friends were listening in, having moved in close behind the steed to hear Poker's response to the confrontation. Once again, all burst into laughter. Rev just hung his head in defeat, his lips forming a quirky grin. He brushed past Mau, and said, "Catch you later; I need some quiet time."

It took a while before the fish calmed down, this being one of Poker's best improvisations. Little Peetie had been hanging out with Uncle Gnarls and his family when this episode began. Bohunk asked Peetie, "Is Poker always like this?"

"Pretty much," came Peetie's reply; "however, if you are in danger, he is the one who will put it all on the line to help. You might say that for Poker, life is nothing more than a playground. Whatever happens, he keeps his outlook positive. You know, in some ways, when you extract his zaniness, he is so much like your dad. He is fearless and does not hesitate to get involved when someone is in trouble. Believe me, the more you get to know that crazy swordfish, the more you will appreciate him. And as a bonus, he *will* keep you laughing."

Mau was trying hard to gather his composure, his side hurting from laughing so hard. He motioned Socrates away from his group of friends. Swimming over to the opposite side of the bay from where the humans were staying, Mau said, "I need to introduce you to that stallion. However, this time we cannot include Poker in the conversation. He never stops---I swear, I am going to die from laughing so hard. How do you deal with him?"

"The best way is to send him on a mission. That way, you can be as serious as you like, at least, until he returns."

"So, he's … like, um, hopeless?"

"Well, if you are talking about his wit … yep, he is pretty much hopeless. However, you will never find a truer friend."

Socrates and Mau waited for a little while before searching out the big stallion. Having found him, Socrates opened the conversation; "It is a privilege to meet you. I am Socrates."

Rev stared long and hard at Socrates, a bit confused, he thinking from the incredible stories of his legacy that the DK cod was bigger than life. Mau broke the brief silence, addressing Rev; "Look, old friend, we have a problem. Let me explain our circumstances and, please, let us know if you can help."

Rev listened, however he was letting his bias of smaller species of fish affect his opinion of Socrates. He did not pay much attention to what Mau was sharing with him such as how Socrates and Poker were managing to effect an incredible interaction between all varieties of ocean inhabitants as well as conquering the divide between fish and humans, an example being what just happened on the other side of the web. Rev's arrogance finally triggered a snide response, addressing Socrates; "Why should any of us care about those things? I have seen it all … and to tell you the truth, '*little fish'*, I personally have never known anyone who gives a rip about how *anything* affects *anyone* else!"

Socrates grimaced, his steely stare causing the stallion to hackle up in defiance. The big cod's reply was cold: "Who do you think you are, prancing around as though you are some … 'monarch of the sea'? You are no more important than any other creature inhabiting this ocean. Furthermore, you can agree to help us … or you can get your curly tail out of here! We are equipped to handle our circumstances regardless of your choice!"

Rev's nostrils flared wide. Socrates' muscles tightened, his lips rolling back over his massive jaws revealing razor sharp teeth. Mau moved in close to Socrates' side, indicating his choice of support. The big stallion's rage was ramping up and ready to explode, his anger enforced by his opponents united opposition to his self-imposed sovereignty. Mau moved forward, getting in Rev's face; "All the time of our growing up … I thought *you* were bigger than life. Wow, what a disappointment. Tell me; are you too scared to get involved or … are you really just *a 'royal wuss'*?"

Rev reared high; "What did you say? Are you looking for a *fight?* I will give you a *fight!*"

Mau's response, "Which one of those mares are you going to use to do your dirty work?"

This time the stallion charged, the plesiosaur quickly pinning him to the floor of the bay, the sea horse's tail flailing wildly in an effort to strike anything within reach. That is until Socrates locked his jaws on the soft underside of his opponent's neck. A brief moment later, Rev's body went limp, the swift defeat leaving him powerless. Sensing his surrender, Mau eased up though feeling sickened by the conduct of his old friend, concluding; "No one needs to know of this. Now … take your herd and get out of here!"

Squirming out of the clutches of Mau and Socrates, Rev was trying to hold back tears of humiliation. Socrates sensed the seahorses' inexplicable embarrassment and broken spirit, speaking apologetically; "I am sorry; we do not mean you any harm. It is just that---what we have been through lately has been tough, and we need all the help we can get. Please, take your leave; there will be no hard feelings."

Rev turned away, swimming a short distance, for once in his life reflecting on the folly of his arrogance. Socrates and Mau slumped in disappointment, thinking the matter was over. However, Rev swam back, re-engaging them: "Look,

I … uh, do want to help. Let me know what you need; my herd is at your disposal."

Impressed by the reversal of the stallion's initial response, Socrates and Mau once again explained their current circumstances, imploring Rev for ideas on where they should proceed from here.

On shore, Ben, Sam, and Buddy sat staring out into the bay, feeling perplexed over what was going on with the fish. The bay was now quiet; however, their mounts seemed to have vanished. Approaching from behind, Malanai kneeled down next to Ben, brushing back his jet-black hair through her fingers and whispering, "They will be back. My Rev knows I am here and he will not go far. However, I am curious about the eruption in the bay; that is something I have never seen before."

Buddy replied, "Well if you ask me, it probably had something to do with all that kelp that washed in earlier. Most of it is gone now. Maybe the stallion and his herd ate it and it gave them all … gas."

Sam and Ben began chuckling while Malanai lowered her head, cupping her face in her hands. Sam said, "Real nice

Buddy; yeah, that must have been what happened; a thousand seahorses suffering from a gas attack. Yep, that had to be it."

Turning her head to the side and giggling, Malanai was wondering if that is actually what happened, having seen her Rev launching completely out of water before expelling a loud, familiar natural sound.

Sam finally stood up; "Let's round up some food. We cannot do a thing until the herd returns anyway, so we might as well use our time wisely. After we eat, I want to swim back out and see if that big cod is still hanging around. I get a strong feeling he is trying to communicate something that will help get us out of here."

Chapter 13

Hearing Rev's accounting of whale songs stunned Socrates. Quizzing Rev he asked, "Where are the sounds coming from?"

"From the abyssal," answered Rev: "they are coming from deep within the abyssal. There is an obvious link to the outside from somewhere far below. However, the songs are audible only from that one place. Its unique spiral into an unfathomable chasm captures and amplifies phantom sounds."

Socrates replied, "How do you know they are ... *whale* songs?"

"I have some friends in the region. They frequently sing to our herd, repeating the songs over and over and explaining them to us. They are the ones sharing the songs about ... *you.*"

Mau then asked Rev, "Are you saying you have … *whale friends,* somewhere around *here?*"

"No, they do not live around *here.* They choose to stay in the region of the abyssal. That is quite a long way from here."

Socrates asked, "What kind of whales are they?"

Rev's face took on the brain dead look Shredder frequently sported when asked a question he was not prepared to answer: "What do you mean … what kind? They are *whales.*" Then spreading his fins out wide and speaking slowly, as though Socrates did not understand, he continued, "That makes them … *big* … whales."

Thinking about what would be going through Poker's mind in this situation, Socrates peered out of the corner of his eyes at Mau, whispering; "Mmmm … somewhere in the neighborhood of a … half-shell short of a clam?"

Mau turned away, his eyes swelling from the urge to laugh.

Socrates then asked Rev, "Can we meet your friends?"

"Sure, however, we will first have to round up my herd. They will be upset if they find out we went without them. The mares love to hear the singing."

Socrates replied, "Not a problem. Perhaps hosting their human riders could also prove beneficial, especially with Schooner and his little friend tagging along."

Rev shrugged, "Sounds good; you know, if we hurry, we can lock into the Harmony current. It is an awesome ride and will save us a lot of time."

Arriving back in the bay, Socrates saw Sam and Ben swimming around as though they were looking for something. He slowly approached the men, circling around and confronting them, catching Ben by surprise. Pushing his hands forward in a reverse breaststroke, Ben pulled up. Socrates swam slowly past, once again swiping his fin across the man's hand. He then turned toward shore, twitching his head, urging the men to follow. Coming back into the shallows, Socrates saw Malanai frolicking around, playing with Chloe and Tooney. Socrates swam in close to Tooney, raising his tail out of the water and splashing it down hard on the surface. Without a second thought, Tooney caught on and began signaling for Schooner to come, the young dolphin instantly racing to Tooney's side. Sam and Ben could sense what this meant; they needed to get ready to ride. Socrates retreated into the bay, seeking out his friends. His instructions were explicit; "Bondar, Two Stars, Zippee, Serine,

I need you to follow me and Mau. Stay close to Schooner and the little boy. Jibber, I need you, Stony, and Rocky to accompany us also. Poker, stay here with the rest and follow Nui's instructions. Kooks and Java can lead you to their secret overlook so you can keep an eye on the enemy. There is no telling what to expect once they regroup. If a problem arises, enlist the help of Kabooga."

Amaya for the first time was perturbed at Socrates; "Well, what about *me?* What am I supposed to do, *babysit?*"

Socrates' face turned pale, realizing he did not even take into consideration the one he loved the most in the world, automatically leaving her out as though her staying with Kaihula's newborns was a foregone conclusion. *"There is no way I am being left out! I am going with you! I am not going to sit idly by while everyone else takes all the risks!"* She then swam over next to Zippee, giving her a fin slap. A united smirk from the girls aimed at Socrates brought a hush from the rest of their group of friends. Poker of course could not help himself, addressing his sidekick: "Whoa, dude, you are swimming in murky water."

Socrates embarrassingly made his way over to Amaya, apologizing; "I am so sorry; yes, you too need to go. The stallion shared something with us that you especially need to be aware of." Then, hamming it up a bit he nudged up against her and whispered, "C'mon doll, you will forgive me … won't you. Give me a little smooch."

Everyone started laughing, seeing Amaya taken back by Socrates' sudden wit. She replied, "You have been hanging out with that crazy swordfish too long!" Then, responding in kind, she surprised him by laying a big kiss on him and saying; "Come on big guy, there is adventure a waitin'."

The laughter grew even louder. Within just a few moments, Rev returned with his herd, their approach just as spectacular as the first time they arrived. On shore, Ben and Sam stood ready, along with all the riders, their excitement building for a romp into the unknown. Malanai swam out first, Rev rearing high as she rolled onto his back. Each rider's mount then followed suit and within moments the Posse was ready to ride. The display was spectacular, Rev and Malanai leading the way, being joined by Socrates and his group of friends. Locking into the surge of the Harmony current, the moderate flow began sweeping them away.

Chapter 14

Nations Pride's arrival came as a welcome relief to Joseph Hawk and his security team, the ship's ability to covertly monitor military satellites making everyone a bit nervous. Helping Joleen disembark the ship, Joseph whisked her and James away to review downloaded images of what his team was busy tracking over the past several hours. James and Joleen took a seat, both leaning forward and focusing intently on the massive imagery of the thirty-foot screen. Joseph took control of the remote, speeding up events to save time. Immediately after Nations Pride's launch from the island, the military vessels sped away, being alerted to a strange unidentified space craft flying within twenty miles of their island. "Look at that thing!" Joseph shouted, "What is that?"

James and Joleen broke into laughter, Joleen getting out of her seat, giving Joseph a big hug and replying, "That, my brave chieftain is a Clingon War Ship. Pretty impressive, isn't it?"

Joseph's previously panic stricken face slowly melted into a stoic stare followed by a nod of his head and a big smile of approval: "Mmmm … good trick."

All present in the security office broke into laughter, knowing the skeleton crew onboard Nations Pride managed to fake out two military warships and a nuclear sub. Joleen allowed a few moments for savoring the brief victory, knowing their fight had just begun. Taking Joseph aside she directed, "Get everyone on the island to our amphitheatre. We have to consider our strategy."

Addressing her audience, Joleen Teal did not mince any words, the tone of her voice reflecting her fervor for getting things done: "My friends, we have to prepare for a fight. Our discovery in the Triangle is at risk. The United States military is obviously on high alert and we cannot allow their interference. We are going to have to do everything we can to distract them until our ship's crew can retrieve the four members of our team still lost out there. All outside activities are hereby suspended. We have enough supplies to provide for our needs for several months. Let us use them wisely. Joseph Hawk will advise each group with their task assignments after a meeting with our security team. Now, for those perhaps wondering, including Joseph, the answer is … *no*; for now our operation will not require war paint or dancing around fires."

A muffled wave of laughter rippled across the tropical outdoor gallery, Joseph nodding his head in approval of Joleen's approach to a difficult situation; seriousness balanced with wit, keeping the mind sharp.

Ms. Teal and James hastened back to the New Technologies lab. Charlie arrived just moments later with the two young Indian maidens who previously presented him with the crate containing the uncut diamond. Charlie's face was glowing with excitement over their progress in such a short time. Having simply sketched his proposed idea for the diamond and presenting it to the islands stonecutters, the team of artisans quickly wrote a computer program for the parameters that Charlie insisted would work.

Placing opposing ends of the huge stone into the grip of a computerized facet cutter, the process began. Tracks of intense light were shooting through and around the rotating rough stone to the tune of several hundred times per minute, stopping only briefly to tap when detecting a perfect angle. Standing on a small balcony overlooking the procedure, Charlie was staring in amazement at the intensity of the artisans' rapt attention to every procedure, constantly monitoring the machine's activity to prevent any mistakes. The passing of hours flew by quickly, the cutting of the diamond mesmerizing all in the lab as the stone took shape. Halfway through the process, the stone's light reflection was growing so intense that a lab assistant had to pass out special eyewear to prevent damage to the observers' retinas. Hours later, with cutting complete, a large cushioned platform rose up to support the diamond before releasing it from the machine's grip. Emerging from an oblong chamber was a perfectly cut and faceted stone, the yield of its mass at least twice what Charlie originally expected. Its unique design of a concave capped parallelogram tapering to a multifaceted point stunned even the man who designed it. Charlie glared at the finished product for several minutes before turning to the stonecutters with a tear in his eye; "It is beautiful; it is absolutely beautiful. Thank you."

One of the team replied, "We will accept commendation only when we see it succeed in the task it was designed for."

"Of course," Charlie replied, "yes; for now place it in the vault and take its finished measurements to the Raptor's hanger for proper fitting."

This next step was crucial, Charlie having designed a rotating carriage for housing both diamonds, the original with its modified multifaceted cone tip, and this new version employing Charlie's original design for light infusion, having the capacity to implode atoms, bonding their nucleus with their network of electrons and protons, the subsequent chain reaction shrinking a targeted object to microscopic proportions. However, the capacity of this new version's design was far more intense, hypothetically causing very large objects to disappear.

For the next several days, the Raptor's design team patiently worked on refitting the aircraft to employ the new technology, giving Joleen and James time to think about what to target, the warrior side of Joleen's personality determined not to waste the test fire. Her angry eyes were busy scanning their beautiful three dimensional world globe in the New Technologies lab, the image rotating continually. Going through her mind were the latest news reports of global terrorism, human trafficking, and corruption in every sector of human society. She began thinking, 'There is nothing left worth saving'. However, her thoughts of Sam, Buddy, Chloe, and Tooney brought her mind back to their immediate task; rescuing their friends. Yet, she could not control her thoughts drifting back to Sam's conclusion: target the root cause of the world's madness, the religious fervor causing it. Her face took on an indignant grin, suggesting to James; "We need to start thinking like Sam. In order to rid our world of the blight afflicting it, we have to address the source of the problem. You *know* what that is. And, if anyone *dares interfere*, they too can … *disappear!*"

James understood her frustration yet cautioned; "Joleen, I understand how you feel. However, there is no need for us to involve ourselves with that particular target."

"Well, it makes perfect sense to me! Why shouldn't we attack the source?"

"Because … the plans for what you want to do are already on the table."

Joleen cocked her head sideways, curious as to what he meant by that statement.

James continued, "Over the past several years I have been privy to classified information involving something that security advisors employed by the United Nations are working on. Most members of that international body feel the same way you and Sam do, with sentiment growing to start withdrawing legal charters from all organizations who stir up public dissent. Leaders have had it with the overwhelming divisive hypocrisy they feel is choking international cooperation. Centuries of impropriety including rubbing elbows with politicians and greedy commercialists in order to keep one's position in the worldwide political arena secure cannot forever be tolerated. Current assumptions suggest that a removal of clerical influence will result in an easing of world tensions. Believe me Joleen; the planning phase is almost complete. My suggestion to you is to allow it to play out. Instead, I think we should re-visit Chloe's idea; test fire on North Korea and Iran, this time targeting their nuclear sites with Charlie's new laser. The disappearance of those facilities will certainly stir up the international community. And just think of the satisfaction it will bring us when our Raptor puts a choke hold on the rogue nations, to say nothing of the fear it will infuse into others, having a phantom lurking in unknown places."

Joleen's countenance began softening, nodding approval of James' sage advice and replying: "Thank you cousin. I am sorry to appear so angry. Please share your thoughts with Charlie and Joseph. I need to get back to my lodge and calm down a bit. I really need some sleep."

Just then, Corey Coulson burst into the room: *"Hold onto your hats people, we have a visitor. Quick, follow me to the ship."*

James and Joleen boarded a tram and took off with the young helmsman. Upon boarding Nations Pride, Corey replayed some of the video taken of their latest mission, narrating its content: "This begins when we started uploading information into the military satellite. Okay, we see the ships and the sub in the periphery. Now, what else do you see?" Pointing to an obscure object in the water adjacent to the sub he asked, "What, pray tell, is that?"

James and Joleen's eyes were tightly squinted, the object faintly perceptible. Corey gave them a moment before clearing its definition. "*What in the world,* Joleen blurted out, *"That's our whale!"*

"It sure is," Corey replied, "with a whole in its fluke and everything. That critter has obviously been dogging us since we left the area of the caverns. Here, let me show you more of the video."

For the next hour, Corey shared images of Big Jake staying close to Nations Pride. "I cannot believe I didn't notice him before. We were so intent on everything going on with the military ships; I guess we overlooked the big guy. Thinking back, he did peel away from the other fish when you and Sam entered the cavern. The only sense I can make out of this is … he is hanging around to help with our next move."

James stood quiet for a moment, gathering his thoughts before asking; "How could he possibly follow us? Our ship is virtually invisible and there is nothing we know of that can penetrate our cloaking defense. Corey, scan our perimeter."

"What am I looking for sir?"

"Look for anything compromising our hull."

Scanning every inch of Nations Pride, nothing showed up. James' head was rolling from side to side, his curiosity building; "How is it that he can follow what he cannot see or hear?"

Joleen suddenly slapped the table, startling the other two; "I've got it: It has to be the simple pressure of our ship's exhaust. Nothing else can detect it, but I will bet you our whale can, especially, if he stays close in our wake. He must have a sensory organ of some kind that can pick up even the slightest anomaly. What do you say we get out of here and try to find him?"

Corey shrugged and nodded in the affirmative, James replying, "Okay; however, we need to check with security to see if any military vessels are still patrolling this region."

James quickly took off to meet with his security team while Corey and Joleen stayed onboard for necessary systems checks. It took only moments for the 'all clear' and James made haste back to the ship. Once onboard, James had a question for Corey; "Before we take off, through all of what we saw on the screen, have you reviewed any audible?"

Corey's eyes slowly closed as if he just failed a test. "Oh man," he replied, "what is wrong with me?"

He quickly restarted the video, speeding up the process by putting it on audio tracking, targeting only moments of unusual sound detection. From time to time, the distinct sound of a humpback whale would interrupt the silence, like the call of a love-starved loon across a fogged in lake. "It has to be him," Corey suggested, "because typically, only males of the species vocalize and we have no other readings of humpbacks anywhere on this video."

However, closer to the end of the recording, Corey detected something new: "Wow, check this out. Listen; do you hear it?"

Corey began increasing the volume and clearing the definition, honing in on a series of clicks. Some patterns were repetitive, others distinctly different. A smile swept across his face; "Beautiful isn't it? What you are hearing is a coda, a song orchestrated by a pod of female sperm whales. Their communication is like no other on the planet." Corey stopped the recording in mid song, reversing the audible, playing it again: "Listen to the unique repetitive patterns of three to five clicks in succession ramping up to a melody from multiple voices harmonizing in a volley of up to twenty clicks. The only times these patterns are used are in social situations. We are listening to an opera." Leaning back in his chair and clasping his hands behind his head, Corey closed his eyes in order to take in the full impact of the harmonious melody. Within the next minute however, his chair fell back, causing him to smack his head on the floor. Jumping to his feet he stopped the audio, backing it up and replaying the previous twenty seconds. In the midst of the melody, the song of a humpback whale interrupted. However, at that point, the codas grew even more intense. Joleen, Corey, and James began looking at each other in amazement, Joleen responding, "Is our humpback communicating with the other species?"

Corey's eyes were wide open with wonder; "How cool would that be? I for one want to find out. Let's get this show on the road."

Once again, Nations Pride submerged, making its way through the subterranean channel and into the South Atlantic. Setting his autopilot to track the same GPS co-ordinates to the location of the highest intensity codas, Corey also cranked up their audio monitors so as not to miss anything. However, his excitement level began slowly tapering off when an hour passed without hearing a single sound. The crew was not only getting bored but was also weary from a lack of sleep, Corey finally dozing off from sheer exhaustion. Suddenly, while only ten minutes into his restful snooze, something bumped Nations pride, causing the vessel to list hard to port. Joleen shouted, *"What is happening?"*

Corey was struggling to compensate to starboard, all the time scanning their hull for the source of the impact. Having steered clear of the object for but a moment, he quickly threw the ship's thrusters in reverse, his vision trained on the full-grown humpback they had been looking for on a collision course with the bow of the ship. Only a split second from a head on collision, the mammoth suddenly pulled up, heading straight for the surface and breaching completely out of the water. Taking a moment to breathe, the great whale immersed once again, this time propelling himself in slow circles around Nations Pride. Joleen whispered to Corey, 'What now?"

"I do not know."

James gently grabbed on to Joleen's hand, turning her toward him, "I have an idea; you were in the water with that creature in the Triangle. Why not re-acquaint yourself with him?"

"What are you saying? You want me to go out there all alone with the behemoth that just *rammed our ship?*"

"Joleen, he nudged our ship; if he wanted to harm us, that obviously would not be a problem. Look at him."

Joleen trained her eyes on the whale, the gentle motion of its great flippers seemingly enticing communication. Corey urged her, "Ms. Teal, you of all people believe in what Tooney started. Who knows, maybe this is our shot at getting our friends back. Let's surface; it is worth a try."

After a moment of quiet contemplation, Joleen nodded and Corey raised Nations Pride to the surface. James opened the hatch while Joleen changed into her diving gear, this time using only a swimsuit, mask, snorkel, and fins. Big Jake slowed in his movement, staying about twenty feet away from the ship. Joleen was feeling half scared out of her wits from not knowing what to expect. Easing off the dive platform and into the water, a strange sense of euphoria enveloped her, her heart rate slowing as she propelled forward with a gentle kick of her fins. Approaching Big Jake from his left side, she took off her dive mask, her long dark hair swaying like lace in the current, her stunning blue eyes peering deep into his. Big Jakes' left eye slowly closed as if taking a photo snapshot of this beautiful creature. Joleen then began sliding her hands across his head before caressing him with her arms. Moving further back, she grabbed on to the foreside of his left flipper, holding on tight as he pushed down, carefully propelling forward, and submerging only about twenty feet before floating effortlessly back to the surface. What happened next caught them both by surprise. Using nautical speakers designed into the hull of Nations Pride, Corey replayed the audio from the codas, including Big Jakes brief interlude. Joleen let go the powerful flipper, moving forward to the side of his head, peering once again into the darkness of his eye, the opera of song tantalizing her spirit into a waltz with the magnificent, docile giant. Locked in Joleen's embrace, Jake rolled over slightly on his side, lazily tapping the water with his left flipper, spinning the two in a slow circle of profound ecstasy. When the codas concluded, Joleen could not move, her senses frozen in the hypnotic moment.

The silence that followed was brief, the codas mysteriously resuming, this time from the depths below, their intensity ramping up. Big Jake was careful to respond, Joleen still clinging to his side. Rising from the deep was an entire pod of sperm whales, their graceful movement rivaling a perfect ballet, their accent to the surface beginning to unfold like the miraculous rapture of the birth of a flower. After releasing her grip, Joleen put both her hands to her mouth, throwing a kiss to her partner before making her way back to the ship. In a final display, Big Jake began racing to pick up speed, once again breaching high in a grand conclusion, and diving straight through the heart of the emerging blossom, disappearing through its petals like a phantom spirit of ages past.

Chapter 15

Back on board Nations Pride, Joleen, James, and Corey uttered not a word for some time, their response impaired by the whales' incomprehensible display of power, harmony, and beauty. Corey spoke first; "There has to be something significant to the codas. I have never heard anything remotely resembling this interchange. The big humpback has to be trying to tell us something. We need to lure him back."

Corey began replaying the audio of Big Jakes song, the ecstasy of the shrill notes tickling the psyche like an excited parent hearing the first whimper of their newborn child.

Only moments later, Big Jake once again stormed to the surface, breaching high, this time only to show off for the pod of female sperm whales. "So, what do you think ladies? Was that awesome, or what?"

The females started giggling, absolutely loving their interchange with the cavalier humpback. "C'mon girls, you can help out Big Jake, can't you? All I ask is that you take us to the entry of the lost world you keep telling me about, the place where you are hearing requests for your songs."

One of the females responded, "It is too deep for you. There is no way for you to survive."

Jake thought about her answer; she was right. Humpbacks can only hold their breath for half or less than what these girls can. The sperm whales can also dive at least ten to twenty times deeper. However, he began wondering if the ship might have the capacity to submerge to such depths. He had an idea but would have to hurry as the female pod spends very little time on the surface.

A shiver ran up the spines of the crew of Nations Pride, an inexplicable force surrounding their ship and dragging it down. Grabbing the yoke at the helm in a panic, Corey cried out, "Oh boy, something has a hold of us! Hang on people!"

Scanning the hull, Corey saw what was happening; "It's the whales; they have us wedged in between them! They are taking us down! Look, look there; it's the humpback taking the lead!"

Locking Nations Pride into their grip, two of the sperm whales were pressing in tightly against the starboard and port sides while another settled in on top once their dive commenced. Big Jake led the way until he maxed out on his air supply, finally peeling away with a wave from his great flippers, another of the females taking over his spot at point. Corey gently notched up the ship's forward power to take control of their momentum. Sensing the change, the whales eased off, allowing Nations Pride the freedom to maneuver. Joleen had a death grip on James' shoulders, the bleakness of the depths beginning to scare her. James finally said, "Hey cousin, take a seat, we will be okay. You know the capacity of this ship. We are safe." He then asked Corey, "When do we turn on the navigational lights?"

"We are okay for now. Light will not help us much until this pod backs off. Right now they have us too tightly surrounded. I am just curious as to where they are leading us."

The ship continued down, Corey trying to scan the area surrounding them, having a difficult time because of the close proximity of the pod of whales. However, reaching the depth of four thousand feet, their escorts scattered, the overwhelming blackness suddenly turning into a world of wonder featuring small marine creatures dancing in a bioluminescent light show rivaling a midnight display on the streets of Las Vegas. Corey quipped, "Well, those girls certainly do have something to sing about."

James asked, "You are recording this, aren't you?"

"Yes Sir; every second of it. I don't get it though. The big humpback cannot even come close to submerging to these depths, so why the need to choreograph this dive? There has to be something more. Sorry, you two, I hate to interrupt the entertainment, but I am going to turn our perimeter lights on now."

The crew gasped when the structure of the abyssal became visible. Fronted with a drop off into an even deeper chasm, the surrounding structure was several thousand feet in circumference with towering circular walls jutting straight up. Corey whispered, "Wow, you do not see something like this every day. It looks as though this gorge's structure is the result of a designed plan. Look, look at the uniformity of the canyon walls; it makes you wonder if a crew of workers chiseled them all by hand."

Corey's heart just about jumped out of his chest when he suddenly heard entirely different codas coming from an area even deeper in the abyssal. Honing in on the sound, he propelled the ship further into the depths. After only another couple of hundred feet a magnificent, shimmering anomaly appeared in the north wall of the seemingly bottomless chasm. It spanned some three hundred feet across and at least two hundred feet high. Corey stationed Nations Pride directly in front, Joleen grabbing his shoulder and squeezing it hard. "Owww," he shouted, "that hurts!"

Joleen released her grip, whispering; "What Sam and the others disappeared into, in the cavern, is exactly what we are looking at. Only, this is much bigger."

James replied, "Yeah, but you said it closed after they plunged in."

"Yes, it did, which makes me wonder why this remains open. Corey, you have all these coordinates locked in the ships memory, don't you."

"Yes maam, every single inch of the place."

"Then get us back to the island. We are going to change our game plan."

Corey held his hand up, stalling the conversation, urging James and Joleen to listen to new codas coming from the direction of the anomaly: "Listen to these voices in comparison to the ones we first heard. There is a difference in pitch. When you listen to humpbacks, they all sound alike. However, sperm whale songs differ in pitch depending on what ocean they inhabit. You might say they sing in the same language, but with unique accents. These songs are from an entirely different pod of whales."

"How far away do you think they are?" Joleen asked.

Corey responded, "Well, we are in what is called a density, or abyssal, zone. Water actually congeals due to the overwhelming pressure at this depth. In this aquatic stratum, hearing these codas from half way around the world is not what one would consider impossible. I guess, in answer to your question; it all depends on---."

"It all depends on *what?*"

"It depends on where you end up once entering the anomaly. The blip we responded to in the triangle seemingly isolates its source to somewhere within several hundred miles of here. The only way to find out is to … plunge in."

Corey looked up at James and Joleen, awaiting their reaction. Leaning on the console, pondering Corey's assessment, James took a moment before offering; "Okay, let's think this through. If we enter and cannot get back, we risk isolating ourselves, perhaps permanently, in an unknown dimensional stratum. Why don't we simply respond to the Codas … in Morse code? The whales will not understand the dots and dashes but maybe, just maybe, Anders Highley, the individual who sent the distress signal in the Triangle, might end up hearing it. Sam also has a recorder built into his wrist communicator. All we can hope for is that what we do triggers a response from one of them. Only, I suggest you dial up the decibel level as high as you possibly can."

Shrugging their shoulders, Corey and Joleen indicated, 'why not'?

For the next few minutes, Corey and James worked out their message, it reading; 'Nations Pride has found a passage … depth of access point is four thousand five hundred feet … having problems with military targeting our island … will attempt to coordinate recovery effort back in original cavern … our big whale came through … stay safe.'

Cranking up the audio to two hundred decibels, Corey repeated the transmission in one minute intervals some two dozen times. There was nothing more for them to do now, but to get back to the island, hoping beyond hope, that their message got through.

Chapter 16

The flow of the harmony current began subsiding as the Posse was nearing the hangout of the singing whales. This area was far away from any shoreline, making Sam O'Brien extremely nervous. The herd fanned out wide, taking their usual positions in preparation of what was to follow. In the distance, Sam noticed an unusual disturbance, something resembling white caps appearing on the surface. It was not long before the cause manifested itself, a large pod of female sperm whales swimming into view. The appearance of white caps soon became obvious to Sam; sperm whale blowholes are set at an angle, their exhalation going sideways instead of straight up, a unique biological trait distinguishing them from other marine mammals. As the pod approached the herd, Rev shook his body hard, Malanai responding by dismounting and urging the other riders to do the same, with the exception of Tooney who was safe on Schooners back. Of course, the humans' curiosity of this type of marine behavior was raising suspicion about what was going on. Malanai motioned for everyone to stay silent and relax, instructing in a whisper; "Simply follow the seahorses' lead."

The intensity level was building, the entire herd gathering in a huge semi-circle, silently awaiting their leaders signal. In a display of raw power, Rev reared high, flexing his mighty chest before diving straight down. He re-emerged a moment later with his head held high, a signal to prepare for the performance. Malanai sensed what was coming, urging Sam and all the riders to hold their breath, put their heads beneath the water's surface, and listen. The enthralling orchestration of codas was magnificent, the whales using a variety of clicks, interchanging the beat much like the unique musical style of the legendary Beatles rock group back in the nineteen sixties. However, in the middle of the songs, Anders Highley suddenly yanked his head above the surface, gasping for air. In an instant, his head was back below the surface, a distinct sound interrupting the codas grabbing his attention. He excitedly swam over to Captain O'Brien, urging him to submerge and listen for what was coming from the background. Sam listened closely. Anders was right; there was a marked difference between the codas of the whales' performance and an amplified repertoire of dots and dashes.

Sam quickly engaged the recorder on his wrist communicator, asking Anders; "Can you make it out?"

Anders submerged once again, yet the sound mysteriously vanished. Disappointed, he looked at Sam and said, "Sorry sir, the sound caught me unawares. I swear it sounded like *Morse code.*"

Buddy was close by Sam, overhearing the conversation and suggesting; "If it is Morse code, there will be a pattern of intervals between transmissions. Let us hope the whales' singing performance is over soon so we can concentrate on what it is you are hearing."

Sam and Anders agreed, taking turns submerging and listening before coming up for air, Anders always staying down the longest, being an amazing free diver. Within only a short interval, the whales took a breather, and lo and behold, the message from Nations Pride rang through loud and clear. Anders had to surface for a moment to catch his breath, though Sam's recorder was capturing every word. When the message once again ended, Anders asked, "Nations Pride; is that not the ship you were on?"

Sam's face lit up, knowing they needed to get back to the bay to decipher the entire message. Sam urged Malanai to try to get her stallion to co-ordinate their return. However, the semicircle of seahorses suddenly split into several sections with Socrates and his friends ending up right in the middle. Sam and Buddy sensed some kind of confrontation and were at a loss as to what they should do. Rev signaled for his herd to stay aside their human riders. He then re-submerged with a message of his own to the large pod of whales fronting him. Urging Socrates forward, he introduced the pod to his newly acquired friend. One by one, the whales swam in close to Socrates, each one taking a close look at the legend who was inspiring their songs. Led by Tooney and Schooner, Jibber, Stony, and Rocky came swooping in, dancing backwards on their tails and bobbing their heads up and down, a soulful display followed by their own cheerful series of clicks and chirps. The whales then began singing an emotional tribute to Socrates and his friends, the seahorses joining in, graciously interpreting the words:

Honoring the memory of his sisters untimely death,
Seeking out remedies to our oceans dying breath,
Yes, how can one solve problems when knowing not the source
Unless you first seek out the wise ones who can help you chart your course
One there is whose spirit is set on all things right
He is supported by a league of friends who join him in the fight.

Socrates, we sing of Socrates

Our inspiration for all that's good

Making our world a better place

As we all know we should

Yes, we have a leader

One who knows wrong from right

Always willing to put it on the line

Even if no one joins the fight

Yet we will battle right along his side

Seeing our world improve

Under the watchful eye of the one we trust

The DK on the move.

As the whales and seahorses began repeating the words for a second time, Amaya swam forward, locking fins with Socrates, her eyes filling with joyful tears, overwhelmed by the song inspired by her most loyal companion. Bondar, Two Stars, Zippee, and Serine could not help but join the chorus, their love for Socrates and Amaya peaking in this emotional moment. The instant they joined in, the seahorses' voices grew even louder, the variety of Piscean tones causing Sam and the Posse into quiet repose. Sam held Chloe's hand tight, their tear-filled eyes focusing on the big cod. Sam whispered to his daughter, "Joleen was spot on with what she said about our world being a shared experience. It is obvious our instincts

BATTLE FOR ATLANTIS

about that big cod are shared by almost every creature in the ocean."

Tightening her grip on her father's hand, Chloe responded, "Daddy, he is so special; he never leaves our side. Deep in my heart I know he is doing all he can to help us. Tooney shared with me the story of his actions on the day you almost lost the Ocean Gem. He was the one who coordinated the saving of Tooney's life. Malanai also shared with me that he and that swordfish he hangs out with are the ones who led the charge in freeing Ben and his friends from their captors. What we need to figure out is … how can we help them?"

Malanai agreed, stating; "From times long past, there have been stories of special connections with other creatures not of our own kind. I know this because I share a similar spirit, a special bond of adventure with my Revelator. What we are witnessing is a unique display of gratitude, expressions directed to an individual who is affecting others in ways too wonderful for us to comprehend. However long these songs continue, we need to be patient and wait until they conclude. Our attentiveness will be our way of adding dignity to the occasion."

The chorus continued for some time, finally ending with the docile giants disappearing into the deep. Rev then

119

signaled his herd as the Posse mounted up, the Harmony current beginning its reverse flow and gently sweeping them all away. Socrates and his friends decided to stay close to Sam and Chloe, trusting their instincts that what just happened made the necessary connection.

Chapter 17

Nations Pride's emergence in the subterranean channel was a welcome relief to Joseph Hawk, the big man standing on the bank patiently awaiting Ms. Teal's return. Disembarking the ship, the first thing Joleen noticed was an unusual look of anxiety on Joseph's face. She asked; "Is everything okay?"

With a sweep of his arm, Joseph motioned the crew to the tram. Never had Joleen seen Joseph this nervous. Arriving at the facility housing the war room, a team of Joleen's most trusted advisors stood ready with their latest intel, directing her attention to a monitor featuring current activity off the west coast of her island. Two U.S. battleships were cruising up and down the island's coastline. These new ships were smaller than their antiquated counterparts, but Joleen knew from early reports they were far more agile and deadly. The question now was; without notification, what are they doing within the boundary of designated Native American sovereign territory? She immediately called for Joseph to bring James up to date on their security strategy designed to counter intruders. James listened attentively before giving Joleen a cold stare, there being a set strategy for repelling opposition not previously shared with him. In an irritated tone of voice he asked, "What is going on, *cousin?* Is there anything else I need to know? Why did you not brief me in the beginning about something like this? You are the one who made me Chief of Security Operations for the island!"

She answered, "My daddy always told me to keep at least one extra arrow strapped to my quiver, just in case of an unexpected situation. Aside from that, how was I supposed to know how long you would commit to our research? Do not feel bad; this is the only thing I kept from you. Therefore, you and Joseph need to get going. For our plan to work we need *focus.*"

Joseph smiled while exiting the room, admonishing James, "Do not be offended by your cousin's caution. She follows closely in the footsteps of her father. You know as well as anyone how she kept her ear attentive to his wisdom, inclining her heart to discern his sayings. That is why her understanding of the world around her is far superior to most individuals. She uses what is necessary for any given situation, always with the intention of giving more in return. Think back to those days when you two sat in your uncle's lodge in the evenings, listening to his stories?"

James did recall Joleen's rapt attention to her father anytime he uttered even a single word. There was no further need for consideration of this matter.

Joseph and James met up with a group of young scouts who led them down a jungle path to a hidden cove on the southwest side of the island. An extremely dense canopy of trees was obscuring a small river feeding the cove. Coming into view, some two hundred yards up the waterway, was a fleet of twenty well-equipped fishing boats, each individually moored in its own slip along a dock some one hundred and fifty yards long. They were all the same make and model; Boston Whalers, 320 Outrage, all fitted with Hi-Def GPS and depth finder, specialized radar equipment, as well as a top of the line fishing package. Their logos varied in design, sporting symbols of contributing Native American Tribes. The vessel James and Joseph chose to board featured the logo of a peace pipe with the blade of a tomahawk opposite the tobacco bowl, the image criss-crossed with a bow and arrows identifying it as the symbol of the Choctaw Nation of

Oklahoma, the wide circle surrounding the logo reading …
'Chahta Sia Hoke'; translation … 'I am Choctaw'. The team
of young scouts quickly fired up their engines, casting off
their dock lines and beginning a wake-less idle down the
river. Once arriving in the cove, they faced a vicious shallow
bar, the tide rolling in with swells only four to five seconds
apart and rising ten to fifteen feet high, causing a daunting
half-mile trek before reaching safer water into the open ocean.
Once clear of the danger, they powered up to thirty-five knots
on a heading due west.

Within three miles of the coast, their radar indicated that
the military had a lock on their position and was on a vector
to intercept. The scouts changed course, fanning out wide in
a strategic formation, surrounding both battleships within
minutes. This maneuver stunned the military crewmembers,
forcing them into combat readiness. The boat James and
Joseph were on approached the lead ship, James hailing its
Commander on his radio, speaking in the Choctaw language:
"Chim oka peni chito yvt Hattak Vpi Homma isht im ahalaia
chukoa tuk. Nana chim ahni kvt anoli." ("Your vessels have
entered a sovereign Native American research boundary. State
your purpose.")

To James' amazement, the reply was also in the Choctaw language: "OPS ibafoka e hoyo hosh, apela e chim asilhha hosh pa e la." ("We are here to request your help in locating members of a special OPS team.")

Surprised by the answer, yet recognizing the voice as being that of his uncle Nathan, James replied, "Seal Hannail Ibafoka isht ish anumpoli ho?" ("Are you speaking of seal team six?")

Nathan Teal replied this time in English with a slight chuckle in his voice and whispering out of earshot of the ship's personnel; "That would be affirmative. You know how elusive these Special OPS types are after dealing with pirates, often seeking a break on a secluded island for a little R and R. By the way, the military is curious over a pirate captain's report of a UFO targeting his ship with a beam of light. The Navy commanders who rounded up the survivors are also baffled, classifying the light's source as an unexplainable phenomenon and have decided to explore the region. We need an audience with my daughter. With your permission, my wife and I would appreciate an opportunity to surprise her. We also request temporary harbor for these ships off your coast."

Before James could reply, Joseph put his hand over the microphone, cautioning him, "We return with only two boats. The other eighteen are to remain with the military ships until we get a full report of what is going on. Trust is the key ingredient in matters such as this. It is best to keep our quivers full and our scouts on high alert."

James took the words of caution to heart, knowing from Native American history the lies and deception used to put an indigenous people on a 'trail of tears'. They were not worried about Nathan Teal; their concern was with the military escort. James nodded to Joseph that he understood before replying to his Uncle's request; "We are honored to welcome you. Our scouts will guide the ships to calmer water and stay close to communicate any additional requests. Please accept our hospitality."

Immediately, a large platform began its descent from the starboard side of the lead battleship. James began tearing up at seeing his aunt for the first time in at least a decade. Cheyenne Teal's beauty was ageless, her long beautiful hair starting to gray, yet was shimmering in the glow of the sun. Her eyes were the same deep blue of her daughter's, her quiet grace emitting an aura of peace. Never losing sight of her roots, she was dressed in a beautiful full length beaded dress, a dignified example of discreet feminine attire. Taking her hand as she boarded the Whaler, James could not help but give her a big hug. Nathan said, "Hey, what about me?"

James smiled while asking Joseph, "You mind helping my uncle? I am, uh, preoccupied."

Uncle Nate's comical shrug sparked a chuckle from Joseph and the four young scouts piloting the boat. However, a tear started trickling down James' face while in the embrace of his aunt. Memories of his family's past flooded his mind, Cheyenne's presence somehow bridging years of absence from his beloved home of Broken Bow, Oklahoma. He could not wait to see Joleen's reaction to her mom and dad. At the same time, he was hoping beyond hope that they would be able to provide additional balance to the stressful decisions their daughter was currently facing. After getting their guests comfortably seated with life belts properly fitted, the boat quickly accelerated on a heading directly to the southwest tip of the island, getting out of sight of the ships before doubling back and heading for the cove.

Once docked, two of the scouts accompanied Joseph, James, Nathan, and Cheyenne along a jungle trail to the secret entry of the island's headquarters. Joleen was still working with her advisors, forming a strategy as to how to proceed back into the Triangle for a rescue. Joseph quickly rounded up the two young women that previously helped with the diamond container, instructing them to help

Cheyenne freshen up before presenting her to Joleen. The young women were ecstatic, having heard stories of the most beautiful Choctaw princess who ever lived and realizing she was standing right before them. They hurried Cheyenne away to a special lodge, one that Joleen designed for her parents just in case they ever decided to come to the island. Surrounding the communal sitting area in the middle of the circular structure were six tripods supporting large paintings drafted from pictures of Joleen and her parents, each representing different stages of their life on the reservation. Cheyenne's emotions began welling up, the display caressing her heart with the recognition of her daughter's love for their family. After acquainting Cheyenne with the amenities of the lodge, including a wardrobe of beautiful attire hand made by island tailors, the two young women, Molly and Bonnie Mae, waited outside. Twenty minutes later, Cheyenne requested their assistance for a few moments to help her with choices of what jewelry to wear, the large variety of necklaces, bracelets, and headbands making her selection a bit overwhelming. Cheyenne was not a vain woman, yet she appreciated the thrill this reunion was bringing to these young maidens and did not want to spoil their fun.

Arriving at the lodge, Nathan Teal came near to fainting at the sight of his dear wife, his legs buckling, his heart fluttering like a sixteen-year-old high school kid processing the sparkle in the eye of an interested young lady for the first time. He gently took Cheyenne's hand, pulling it forward and kissing it, saying, "You are more beautiful in this moment than in the forty years we have spent in each other's arms. I love you."

Blushing in front of young Molly and Bonnie Mae, Cheyenne responded to her husband, "I love you too, however" --- sniffing the air she added, "I believe it is definitely your turn."

Molly and Bonnie Mae began giggling, Nathan nodding his head in agreement.

Nathan came out only fifteen minutes later, his dear wife nodding once, signaling her approval of his chosen attire; beaded buckskin shirt and trousers, his head crowned with a full royal headdress. Following their escorts, they silently entered the war room arm in arm, Joleen's back to the door, her attention focused on a large monitor mapping out her team's ideas for their next mission. Joseph cleared his throat, suggesting, "Perhaps we should consider the sage advice of our new counselors."

Joleen's head dropped out of sheer frustration, the mood in the room too intense for any advice from newbies.

Turning around, she saw Joseph, James, Molly, and Bonnie Mae standing about fifteen feet from the door, irritatingly spreading her hands and asking ... *"What?"*

Just then, the foursome stepped aside, Nathan and Cheyenne facing their daughter in royal attire. Joleen shrieked, sprinting across the room into her parents' arms, tears of joy flowing down her cheeks while locking herself in their embrace.

Joseph motioned for all staff members to leave the room, allowing Joleen time to reminisce with her mom and dad.

The impact of her parents' presence had an immediate calming effect on Joleen's frustration. Dealing with a rescue mission, as well as her island residents' struggle to keep their discovery in the Triangle a secret, was causing her stress level to ramp up by the minute, and bringing her close to an emotional breakdown. Leading her folks across the room to a secluded sitting area, she sat between them on a large couch and began sobbing: "Oh daddy and mom, thank you for coming. I cannot believe what has been unfolding in just the short time since our meeting in Florida. Let me fill you in."

Joleen took at least an hour to bring her parents up to date on what was happening. Her parents were enthralled, though not necessarily surprised, at her account of the interchange with the big humpback and the pod of female sperm whales. Especially intriguing to them was hearing about how James used Charlie's new computer program to trick the U.S. Military by uploading bogus information from Nations Pride into a satellite. Nathan and Cheyenne sat quietly, carefully listening to every detail of Joleen's assessment of the difficulties her island residents were now facing. She concluded, "I need you so much right now. Please say you will stay and help."

Wrapping her daughter tight in her arms, Cheyenne whispered; "There is no power on earth that could pull us away in your time of crisis."

Nathan lightened up the moment, asking, "Where is Joseph? I need *war paint!*"

Joleen and her mom busted out laughing, Nathan's wit being the perfect balance for this overwhelming situation.

Joleen then jumped to her feet, rushing out of the door and giving her staff instructions to prepare for an official Pow-Wow.

Chapter 18

While arrangements for the gathering were in progress, Joleen introduced her parents to Charlie and Carlynn, the couples feeling an almost instantaneous connection. Joleen excused herself after escorting them to a sitting area along the banks of the river. Charlie and his wife recounted their entire experience starting with the Ocean Gem's near disaster. Nathan and Cheyenne listened intently to Charlie's explanation of Tooney's social progress and how everything the world could possibly throw the boy's way ended up being a simple game, facing even the most difficult of circumstances with fearless instinctual confidence. Charlie concluded with a tear dribbling down the side of his face; "And now he is lost in another ... dimension ... and for some reason we are not overly concerned. Is there something wrong with the way we feel?"

Nathan took his wife's hand, the two looking into each other's eyes and smiling prior to Cheyenne's response; "We have a daughter, named Joleen, and for some reason we feel the same as you. The purity of her spirit has led us to that place where parents trust overrides fear of circumstances. Right now, those lost with your son are fortunate he is in their company. Something tells us, *he* is keeping *them* safe."

That simple reply provided a soothing remedy for Charlie and Carlynns' anxiety, the encouragement reminding Charlie of one of Solomon's insightful proverbs: 'Like apples of gold in silver carvings is a word spoken at the right time.'

Two hours passed before James and Joleen re-appeared, escorting the two couples to a commissary for some refreshment. Nathan could still read a lingering anxiety on his daughters face. Taking her by the hand, they set out for a private stroll among the lodges; "What weighs on your mind, my princess?"

"Oh, daddy, what are we going to do? We still have 18 boats and 72 scouts on patrol with those battleships. I am concerned for them."

Her father responded, "I certainly understand your distrust of the military's presence. However, once the evening is over,

I will fill you in on details of what I have learned since our meeting in Florida. In the morning, we can put our minds together to prepare our strategy. Your scouts will be okay. I left instructions with the ships commanders to provide them with sustenance in our absence. For now though, I am feeling hungry. Let us share something light, after which your mother and I would really like to see more of your island before the Pow-Wow. I have often wondered about your use of the Nations' grants.

Joleen wrapped her arms around her father, the two making their way back to the commissary.

Following a varietal snack of fresh sliced fruit and nuts, Joleen led her parents to the top of one of the platforms overlooking the entire subterranean facility. Nathan and Cheyenne stood awestruck at the city's beauty and sensible layout. Next, they boarded the tram, Joleen filling them in on the facilities designs and the focus of the island's residents: "Our indigenous population has a single goal; to provide earth friendly technologies for our future. Even though our tribal cultures vary, we share a common appreciation for each other's contribution to the process of harmony and peace. It amazes me how someone as young as Charlie and Carlynns' son can comprehend discoveries as easy as reaching for a glass of water and yet, there are so many who are poised to abuse the value of those discoveries. I feel honored to be among this wonderfully diverse population of dedicated, unselfish individuals who are so completely united in their thinking. We have a battle on our hands, but I can never forget the words of Chief Joseph of the Nez Perce when he laid his weapons down and stated that … 'from this day, I fight no more, forever.' Here we stand, a people united and dedicated to peace, yet struggling from a sickening dread that we will have to face the unthinkable in order to preserve our find. Mom, Dad, there has to be a way to avoid the madness of confrontation."

Nathan pulled his daughter toward him, her head wresting against his powerful chest; "Put your fear away my little one. We will figure out a way. First, though, you need some rest, followed by the heart happy dances of the Pow-Wow. These will release your anxiety and trap some happiness in the dream web of your heart, making peaceful solutions easier to comprehend."

Nothing in the world could have been better for Joleen on this day than the sudden appearance of her wonderful parents. Still resting in the embrace of her father, she could not help but think back to the days of her youth, her mind always racing with ideas for adventure, her loving parents standing at the ready with dignified counsel and sound advice, like eagles preparing their young for flight. Unexpectedly, after only a couple quiet moments, Nathan and Cheyenne realized their daughter had fallen asleep. Sweeping her tired soul up in his strong arms, Nathan carried his princess to her lodge, laying her gently on her bed, being careful not to awaken her. After softly closing the door, Cheyenne motioned for Molly and Bonnie Mae to stand guard, whispering instructions to make sure no one disturb their daughter. The two young maidens hurried to the doorway, taking their position as sentinels, crossing their arms as if poised to repel an enemy. Cheyenne and Nathan were encouraged by the stalwart character of these dear young people.

Chapter 19

Upon awakening four hours later, Joleen freshened up and changed her garments, desiring attire that is more appropriate for an evening Pow-Wow. Her midday rest felt wonderful, her mind experiencing more clarity and far less anxiety. While exiting her lodge, Molly and Bonnie Mae were still standing outside her door with arms folded across their chests as if daring anyone to disturb their beloved mentor. She responded to their presence by giving each a hug and kind response: "Thank you for standing watch. I love you two so much. Hurry now, you need to get ready for the dances. I will round up my parents and meet you two down by the river. I would appreciate you accompanying us for the entire evening. It will be fun."

Molly and Bonnie Mae turned to each other, briefly clasping each other's hands in their excitement before running off to get ready. Joleen found her parents atop one of the observation towers, sitting on a bench and drinking a cup of coffee: "Mom, dad, thank you for letting me get some rest. I feel so much better. Please, let us start by a taking a stroll along the banks of the river."

Arriving at the water's edge Joleen asked, "So, what do you think?"

Nathan and Cheyenne gave each other a 'look', Nathan asking, "About what?"

"About the ship, what else?"

Nathan and Cheyenne began looking around, a sudden chill gripping them from the perception that their child was 'wigging-out'. Cheyenne grasped her daughter's hand and asked, "Are you talking about one of the battleships?"

Joleen looked at her mom with a big smile, pointing at the pier mooring Nations Pride. Nathan and Cheyenne suddenly did notice the ends of dock lines tied to the pier, the other ends curiously dangling in mid air. Nathan asked, "What kind of trick is this?" He then began contemplating what appeared to be a separation of the water, a resulting small eddy forming some one hundred feet down river, blinking his eyes a couple of times before making out the outline of the near invisible craft. Cheyenne's intense concentration also paid off, being curious as to why she could not see a section of the bank of the river on the opposite side. Both of their reactions were similar, a silent glare betraying the wonder seizing their thoughts. Moments passed before Nathan could speak, "So, this … is … Nations Pride?"

Her parent's response caught Joleen by surprise, not immediately thinking about the remarkable invisibility of the vessel. However, in a moment she started snickering, "Yes daddy; after all, those dock lines are not holding the *air* to the pier."

Rolling his eyes, he replied, "Knowing you princess, and of your accomplishments on this island, your being able to harness the air itself would not surprise me."

Joleen then urged them, "Come, I will give you a tour."

Nathan and Cheyenne were speechless as they walked through the vessel's corridors, listening to every detail of Joleen's explanation of the incredible ship's capacity. After a few moments her father stopped and stated; "Tooney … something tells me he had something to do with this."

Joleen's reply, "Can you now see why we have to be so careful? Tooneys' solving of the military's puzzling hypothesis that they have been working on for over twenty years, coupled with his father's engine designs, has hurled us into a completely new era of exploration."

A big smile swept across her father's face, his mind instantly categorizing the use of this vessel for their morning meeting. However, he was in for the surprise of his life, Joleen not yet having revealed to him … the Raptor.

Standing on the pier, awaiting Joleen and her parents, were Molly and Bonnie Mae, both looking strikingly beautiful in their native attire. They were dressed in ankle length, pleated red and yellow dresses with sewn in beaded vests; the design in Molly's being an assortment of turquoise triangles and squares against its yellow background, Bonnie Mae's choice of red highlighting four unique arrowheads cut from jade. Both were wearing knee-high buckskin moccasins. Molly asked Cheyenne, "Can you hear the drumbeats? The Pow-Wow is starting. Follow us, the trail starts just up ahead."

The one-half mile path through a perfectly groomed canopy of jungle foliage made Nathan and Cheyenne feel as if they were walking in a fairy-tale world, Molly leading the way with a lighted torch. Arriving at the site of the Pow-Wow, Nathan and Cheyenne took off running like two young deer, joining in with a group of young ones who were performing one of their favorite circle dances. James, who had already arrived, sneaked up behind Joleen, quickly grabbing onto her hand and pulling her into joining the rhythmic movements around the fire. The lighthearted motions and steps proved to be the perfect panacea for the stress-induced frustration they were dealing with. Hours went by, the combination of dancing, singing, and eating putting all the residents of the island in a joyful mood. The only one feeling a bit on the outs when the dancing began was Corey Coulson. However, young Molly and Bonnie Mae took him aside, explaining the meaning of each dance and helping him to get the rhythm of the beat. Before the night was over, he had not only joined in around the fire, but it was hard for him to stop. From the small bit of Native American history he was exposed to in school, he was now developing an extreme appreciation for the humanity of these dear people. He was feeling a part of the earth, appreciating it more as his home, a special place prepared for man by a benevolent creator. He looked up at the night sky in all its glory, thinking of how our beautiful life-filled planet is travelling through the heavens at over sixty-six thousand miles per hour. He then turned to Molly and Bonnie Mae, who were standing at his side and said; "Wow, I think I get it; this planet is where we are *meant* to forever reside. It is no wonder that my Captain has so much of a problem with the theories and gibberish offered up by evolutionary scientists and religious leaders. He once said that most of what they teach is nothing more than a combination of pre-conceived ideas, guesswork, Greek philosophy, and paganism, like throwing a mixture of garbage into a blender. When you pour it out, it is still garbage but it oozes more easily into the hearts of mentally lazy populations. Then he said he would never stop searching for answers to our world's woes. Our earthly home is obviously part of a unique plan, and he wishes he could get to know personally the one who designed it."

Staring up at the galactic display of stars and constellations, Molly and Bonnie Mae clung to every word Corey was speaking, this young man's expressions opening wider a shared perception locked deep in their hearts.

Morning came quickly, the island residents feeling happy and refreshed. Joleen and her parents, along with Joseph, James, and Corey were all in the war-room by 6:00 a. m., going over maps of their find. Opening the door and poking his head in at about 6:30, Charlie interrupted: "Joleen, we are ready. Would you like to bring your parents along for a sneak peak?"

Joleen nodded, grabbing her parents by the hand and leading them to the tram to join Charlie and Carlynn for a five-minute ride to a huge warehouse. Upon entering the large facility, a crew of workers stood at the ready to reveal their latest engineering marvel. Charlie took the lead, escorting their guests through a serpentine corridor and into the center of a smooth, stone lined, three hundred foot diameter and one hundred foot high, circular structure. A metal platform was resting aside a large covered object in the center of an apparent launching pad. Charlie signaled an attendant and the cover draping the object began retracting, exposing the latest version of the fearsome … Raptor. Nathan and Cheyenne gasped, the aircraft's design sending a shiver up their spines, causing them to clutch each other's hands. It was beautiful, 'nether worldly'. The couple began slowly walking around its perimeter, gazing at every detail. Its arrowhead shape did not surprise Nathan, knowing from scientific tests the superiority of triangular aircraft designs. What threw him were its curved, bumpy outer edges. "I can explain that," said Charlie, noticing Nathan's quizzical stare: "This design repels the friction caused by earth's atmosphere. The earth's magnetic field, coupled with its atmosphere, acts as a shield for our planet. Objects traveling through our solar system progress at an extreme velocity. However, when an object enters our atmosphere, its progress begins stalling because earth's atmosphere provides density in order to protect us. The object thus slows quickly, causing friction to build up to the point that the object usually burns up before reaching our planet's surface. It is much like a semi truck traveling too fast down a steep grade, the friction caused from the applying of brakes causing so much heat that the brakes fail, sometimes catching them on fire. The bumps on the forward edges of our Raptor serve to break up the gaseous molecules forming our atmosphere, allowing the craft to travel at any speed with relative impunity."

Nathan listened intently, the design making perfect sense. Charlie then explained its capacity for vertical takeoff, hovering in mid air, and landing. His biggest surprise was saved for last. Making his way over to a large touch screen computer, he began the process of revealing his new laser. Motioning everyone to the top of large mobile platform some thirty feet from the side of the craft and providing a birds-eye view of the top, Charlie began sending instructions to the Raptor via a joystick. Its hard cover began retracting, exposing the concave top of a huge diamond, the one he and Tooney redesigned for simple light intensity. Then, with a simple touch of an icon, the carriage housing the diamond rotated ninety degrees, a secondary diamond shifting into position and locking into place. The mechanics of the rotating carriage were flawless. Charlie then explained the diamonds designs including molecular implosion, sending a wave of fear up Nathan's spine. Charlie continued his narrative, "Now, my friends, we are ready for a testfire: does anyone have an idea?"

A big smile instantly swept across Nathan's face; "Yeah, how about using it on Congress. With all that they accomplish, who will ever know they are missing."

Laughter filled the air, everyone sharing similar sarcasm over the incompetence of world leaders. Though laughing over the suggestions, Cheyenne had an idea no one was expecting: "How about targeting some Japanese and Russian fishing trawlers. Those nations have been violating international treaties for decades, laws reasonably established to manage oceanic species, preventing their extinction. We can use the Raptor to light them up, scaring them into abandoning ship; then we rotate the carriage and ... poof."

After a brief silence Cheyenne continued; "I am sure we can coax the Admiral into providing us with satellite coordinates. The Navy must know the whereabouts of those vessels."

Grabbing her mother by the arm and spinning her around, Joleen asked in a half-panicky voice; "What *Admiral* are you talking about?"

Nathan calmed his daughter, "Hold on Princess. We were going to get to that. Let's go to the commissary and talk over some breakfast." Then turning to Charlie he asked; "How about you and your wife joining us?" Then directing his attention to James he added; "You and Joseph need to hear this too."

Charlie spent a few moments with his staff getting the Raptor re-covered before joining the others aboard the tram and heading back to the commissary. Once comfortably seated, Nathan explained; "When I got back to Durant after our meeting in Florida, I rounded up some of our tribal elders and had them give Admiral McCauley a history lesson he will not soon forget. The focus of their discussion centered on the last two hundred years of Native American history including the tragic decades-long indignities suffered on a 'Trail of Tears'. Following his lesson, we all gathered for a stickball tournament, his young Lieutenant joining the games. Later in the evening, while sitting around a campfire under the stars, one of our young women, noticing tears in the Admiral's eyes, comforted him by draping a blanket over his shoulders. Then kneeling beside him and taking his hand in hers she said; "Nationalism is a proven blight on mankind. Averting tragedy can be as simple as gaining an accurate knowledge of, and showing respect for, each other's culture. Sometimes even our tribal elders have a problem with this. However, the way I see it is that we Choctaws are just one of earth's many varieties of people whose desire is to share our understanding of the world we know and promote peaceful existence." Overhearing her words to the Admiral made me tear up also. However, I saw in the man a side that had probably been eluding him all his life. In a trembling voice he made a request to the young woman; "In the morning, can you teach me more?" That simple request helped me to realize his heart can be trusted. We allowed him a morning of instruction with the young woman before your mother and I made our request for his help."

Joleen's response was quick and to the point; "So, you finagled two Battleships?"

"No, princess, we simply considered with him a generic, hypothetical situation in order to illicit a reaction. The battleships were his idea. Without a word from us, he made a call, convincing the military that maneuvers in the Atlantic were already scheduled, so why not let him tag along as an advisor. They immediately accepted his offer. Within a half an hour, a military helicopter picked the three of us up, flying us to Oklahoma City where we boarded a plane headed to an Air Force base in Missouri. Our subsequent flight was destined for a land to ship transfer off the Bahamian Coast. It all happened so fast that your mother and I decided to, how do you young ones say; 'Roll with it'? What is funny is that the Admiral is aboard one of those ships off your coast and still does not know a thing about this island, with the exception of it being a Sovereign Native American aquatic research facility. I simply provided him with some co-ordinates and … here we are. His willingness to stick his neck out for us has me convinced he is trustworthy. I think it is time we 'throw the dog a bone'. The man needs something to chew on and he does have oversight of assets that can be put to good use."

Joleen was accepting of her father's counsel yet her agreement came with terms: "What we share with the Admiral will be aboard his ship. The man is not to set foot on this Island or made aware of the existence of our ship or the Raptor. In addition, we will not be sharing one iota of Tooney's discovery with him. Our strategy will be simply to secure our discovery with the ruse of gaining insight into the phenomena gripping the Triangle." Her eyes then took on an icy glare of determination, adding; "I am sorry papa, but I have to ask all of you a very difficult question: *Do I make myself clear?*'"

Nathan and Cheyenne's eyes opened wide, Joseph and James responding with a slight snicker, while Charlie and Carlynn sat up straight nodding affirmatively. Joleen then took a sip of coffee before continuing: "Now that we are all in agreement, we will finish our breakfast and head down to the cove. I am looking forward to an interesting interchange with this ... Admiral McCauley."

Chapter 20

Halfway back to the bay, Malanai tightened her grip on Rev's neck, slamming her heels against his powerful body, causing him to rear high. The entire herd came to a swift halt, the resulting wake swamping the Posse. Ben quickly approached her side; *"What's wrong?"*

Extending her hand she said, "Wait here!" Moments later, in the distance, Ben saw Rev rearing high in the air with Malanai glaring at something on the horizon. His curiosity getting the best of him, Ben took off, galloping away to find out what was going on. Pulling up alongside Malanai, Ben asked, "What is it; what do you see?"

Malanai could not take her eyes off the distant structure, her mind flooding with a sudden wave of horrible memories. Turning to Ben, she urged him; "Please, lead the others back to the bay. I will catch up in a little while."

Ben replied, "Which one of our mounts is capable of taking the lead? None of us know the way back."

Slapping Rev hard on the right side of his neck while letting out an ear-shattering shriek, Malanai coaxed Rev into belting out a commanding bellow, instantly alerting his herd. The stallion Buddy was riding moved quickly to the front, answering Rev with a resounding series of snorts. Buddy held on tight, his mount hackling his neck high, breaking into a commanding strut which signified his acceptance of the role of leadership and taking charge. The entire herd responded by gathering behind the new leader, obediently resuming their course back to the bay. Of course, there was no denying Tooney another opportunity for adventure, he and Schooner breaking away to follow Ben and Malanai, their action eliciting the same response from Sam, Chloe, Anders, as well as a couple of dozen more of the Posse. Ben halfway expected some to follow, saying to Malanai, "Sorry doll, we are a team. Where you go, we go. We will not allow you to face the unknown without support."

Sam and Chloe's approach brought a chuckling response from Malanai, Ben curious as to what she suddenly found humorous. Swimming in close to Sam was none other than ... Socrates and friends, including Mau and the dolphins. Rev suddenly shook his body hard, an indication for Malanai to dismount. Slipping below the waterline, he engaged Socrates; "We are approaching an area that is very dangerous, at least, it used to be. My herd never traverses these waters, the evil inhabitants having claimed half my herd the last time we ventured too close to that distant shoreline. However, I will yield to the direction of my rider, hoping we do not end up in peril."

Socrates thought about Rev's words for a moment, looking over at Mau and Bondar who were listening in, silently imploring their thoughts. Mau raised his head high out of the water, looking far into the distance, curious as to Rev's recollection of the danger. Locating the distant structure, Mau heaved a huge sigh, his head slumping before slipping back beneath the surface. He looked at Rev, the stallion responding; "Bring back memories?"

Mau closed his eyes for a brief moment, shaking his head from side to side, gathering his thoughts before replying: "I always hoped I would never see that place again. If the inhabitants still exist, we will gather our forces and put an end to the horror they spawn!"

Rev re-emerged above the surface, having swooped in beneath Malanai, raising her high. Sam implored her for an explanation, yet she was not ready to reply, at least not without getting closer and verifying that what they were seeing from a distance was actually what she thought it was. She motioned for the riders to follow her for a closer look. Sam however called out, "Wait a minute." Taking off his wrist recorder and handing it to Anders, he gave the young man a quick lesson as to how it works, concluding: "Go, catch the herd. When you get to the bay, decipher the coded message, and wait for our return."

Giving Sam an affirmative nod, Anders and his mount sped away.

Malanai and Rev kept their approach to the distant structure slow and low in the water. Coming into view from the still distant shoreline were definitive terraced walls of an ancient ziggurat, its location fronting a massive cliff. Malanai's emotions began stirring, feeling a sickening dread at the very sight of the pagan temple tower. However, her stern facial expression began softening when drawing closer, seeing the structure's offensive steeple broken off, its crumbled remains lying strewn down the steps leading to its high altar of sacrifice.

Scouring the ocean floor, Two Stars and Bondar happened upon thousands of skeletons piled high, both human and all variety of sea-creatures. Bondar quickly alerted Mau to their discovery, the plesiosaur cringing from his memory of the terror plaguing his ancient home. Seeing Mau's response, Rev also dipped his head beneath the waterline, a sudden panic seizing him when spotting a mass of remains, a great deal comprising those of his friends … all slaughtered simply for sport. He once again raised himself high out of the water, shaking his head violently, his body lurching erratically from obvious distress, Malanai falling into the water and landing hard on her stomach, knocking the wind out of her. Hurrying to her side, Ben tried to lift her onto his mount. She pushed him away, taking a moment to catch her breath before slipping beneath the surface to get a glimpse of whatever it was that set Rev off, gasping the moment she spotted the piled high remains of large seahorses. In that moment, something within Malanai snapped, causing her to swim quickly to Rev's side, motioning for him to lower his head. The great stallion knew the drill, lifting her high out of the water, supporting her torso atop his long snout. For a moment, Rev could not focus, his mind short-circuiting from memories of the ambushing of his herd. Malanai kept his head in a tight grip, the ignition of light from the golden band of glistening triangles in her eyes triggering a quivering pool of fire to form around their emerald core, her intense stare piercing his emotions. The kaleidoscope of colors in his eyes began swirling, their patterns changing with every second, producing sparks that began shooting across his abysmal pupils, a sudden surge of power causing every inch of muscle in his powerful body to flex, forcing Malanai to tighten her grip. Her arms began aching, the interchange taking every ounce of power she could muster, the built up energy of their mind connection finally erupting in an ionic discharge, a small bolt of lightning freezing them in position, and resealing their shared determination. After loosening her grip, Malanai gently kissed Rev's face, the stallion responding by lowering her ever so slowly into the water, the maiden slumping from exhaustion. Ben and his crew of volunteers were in awe once again over Malanai's connection with Rev, the unexplainable interchange leaving the onlookers nearly breathless. Chloe's hands were clutching the hair on both sides of her head, her silence finally broken when blurting out, "I just love that! It is so awesome!" She pleaded with Malanai; "Oh, please, please, please; teach me and my horse to do that."

Malanai held her arms out to Chloe who dismounted, responding instantly to an affectionate hug. Malanai encouraged her, stating; "Little one, a bond like the one I share with my Revelator takes a long time to develop. It starts by getting to know the heart of the one you are building the connection with; leaving no doubt it is someone you can forever trust. It will not always result in visible sparks but, the fire it ignites in your heart is something the two of you will share for as long as you live."

Ben also dismounted, swimming over to Malanai and caressing her, gently stroking her beautiful hair, her head resting on his shoulder, the gentle movement of their legs in the water keeping them afloat. Mau approached Rev and asked; "You, uh, need someone to rest *your* head on?"

Socrates and his friends busted out in laughter, the stallion blinking his eyes and responding; "You wouldn't mind?"

Mau backed away; "Hey, I was kidding."

Rev moved closer to him; "No, I am serious; I really need a hug. Come, give me a hug."

Mau's eyes grew as big as saucers, saying, "Get away from me, you crazy herring ball." Turning to the seahorses, Mau called out, "One of you mares, calm him down! Quick … give him a hug, anything! The sparks have *fried his brain!*"

Just then, Rev winked at Socrates and his friends who instantly caught on to Rev's joke, their laughter causing a quivering disturbance on the water's surface, the seahorses laughing so hard that their riders had to dismount. Rev pointed one of his great fins at Mau and said, *"Gotcha."*

Mau's face took on a frown of embarrassment while nodding his head, accepting the fact that ... *he'd been had*. Rev began strutting his stuff, and chiding, "Yeah, that's right; *who da horse? What*, I can't *hear you*; who ... *da* ... *horse?*"

Mau's embarrassing answer; "Okay, you got me. You; you da horse."

It took a while before the riders could remount, not understanding the sudden erratic response of the seahorses, Malanai even having a difficult time calming Rev down, the stallion cantering around as if he owned the ocean. She finally subdued him by giving him a ... *look*. Rev knew the meaning of ... *the look*. It was a signal for him to obey her order to stop what he was doing and get over here---*fast!*

Malanai then had the Posse gather in a circle, explaining: "What you are seeing on the shoreline is the remains of a citadel; a training facility for the most heinous of warriors. The skeletons you see that are visible on the ocean floor are a reminder of a sick society, individuals priding themselves on killing any living creature simply for sport. If you look closely, you will be able to make out a symbol near the top of the structure, just below the first vertical wall."

All were straining their eyes to try to make out the symbol, Sam quickly recognizing it and turning to Malanai in disgust; "No … not Tammuz?"

Sam's reply caught Malanai by surprise, wondering how he knew who the symbol represented.

Chloe finally blurted out; "Daddy, that looks like a cross."

Sam slumped for a moment before responding to his daughter; "Well, yes … it is. At least, what you see is the symbol that historians say morphed into what we now know as a 'cross.' Its root goes back to Chaldea, close to four thousand years ago: Go ahead Malanai, you explain."

Malanai was curious over what she did not now know of the symbol, however, she continued: "Long ago, there was one who exalted himself to such an extent that he became known as the God of the Sun. He reveled in his being the greatest hater of Almighty God on earth, taking on the name Tammuz, using the idolatrous symbol you are seeing high up on the tower as a visible sign of his self-imposed deification. His original name was Nimrod. There used to be a saying … 'Just like Nimrod, a mighty hunter in opposition to Jehovah.' That reference applied to my own uncle, doing everything he could to keep the legacy of that diabolical murderer alive. My uncle's wicked kingdom reached its zenith when this temple was completed. The skeletal remains you see on the seabed are those of victims he used for training his crony killers."

Malanai's eyes were tearing up, the revulsion of her uncle's infamous legacy wrenching her emotions.

Just then, Ben interrupted, seeing Tooney and Schooner frolicking around only about twenty feet from shore, warning Sam: "The boy needs to stay closer to us until we know the site is safe."

Before anyone could respond, a lone figure brandishing a spear appeared on one of the temple steps. Taking aim, he hurled the missile at his unsuspecting target, cutting a gash in Tooney's thigh and piercing the backside of Schooners dorsal fin. Malanai and Chloe both began screaming, the Posse charging forward to save the child. Socrates and his friends were unaware of what was going on, yet took off after the seahorses charging toward shore. Mau raised his head above the waterline, spotting a lone warrior jumping off the temple wall and breaking into an all out sprint along a trail at the edge of the shore. Mau began speeding ahead to intercept, the great plesiosaur passing the Posse in a flash, timing his target with amazing precision. The very second the man reached his escape route, Mau breached high at the edge of a vertical cliff, whacking the man in the side of his head with one of his massive paddle-like flippers, causing the assailant to fall into the sea. Socrates and his friends still did not know what exactly was going on, at least not until they saw blood oozing out of Tooneys leg and Schooner whimpering in pain. Scooping the perpetrator up in his powerful jaws, Mau swam into deeper water. Coming to a halt and lifting his head high, Mau dropped his prey, the Posse quickly circling and boxing him in. Bondar and Two Stars now made their approach with dorsal fins exposed above the surface, the man's demise obviously eminent. The united show of force caused him to cry out, the horror of his circumstance leaving him begging for mercy. Malanai rode up alongside him: "Ah, Logar, my uncle's snitch! Does it make you feel powerful targeting a young child with your spear? You have only one choice; tell us where you were running to or these sharks will feast on you!"

Writhing in pain, the man cried out, "*The cove,* there is a passage to the other side through a conduit in the back of the *cove!* Your uncle's remaining forces are re-grouping near the web. Your brother has been trying to get them to stop, but they have all rejected his leadership."

Ben looked at Malanai: "Your brother? You mean---"

"I was going to tell you, only, I feel so ashamed."

The warrior continued: "Ashbon, your cousin, is taking control! He wants our slaves back and is in a blind rage over the destruction of the worship column and the 'stone from the stars'!"

Malanai pulled tight on Rev's neck causing him to rear high, her eyes glowing with fire from her outright fury: "What brings you back to this site, *Logar?*"

He defiantly replied, "I was sent ... *for meat!*"

Grimacing from the thought of targeting Tooney and the dolphin for food, the Posse began tightening their ranks, their revulsion of the evil intent causing them to want to kill the man. Malanai and Rev moved forward, getting right into Logar's face, Rev bumping him with his rock hard chest, forcing the perpetrator into a panicky backstroke. The Posse split to allow them passage into deeper water, the evil coward splashing around and gasping for breath, pleading for Malanai to stop. Once several hundred yards offshore, she did stop, concluding the confrontation with words of cold sarcasm: "Okay Logar, now is your chance to find some *meat!*" Pointing toward the open-ocean, she concluded: *"Happy hunting!"*

Flailing in the water, he shouted, *"NOOOO! You cannot leave me out here!"* Tooney and Schooner came racing forward, positioning themselves between Malanai and Logar, the man suddenly lunging at Tooney in a vicious attempt to use him as a hostage. Tooney and Schooner kept backing away, staying just out of reach, the pulsating blood oozing from Tooneys leg forming a pool of red that began swirling around the man's body. A wave of disgust swept over the little boy's face, giving the man a final salute and responding with chilling firmness: *"Yeah, happy hunting!"*

Tooney and Schooner then retreated to Malanai's side. Gnashing his teeth at them, Logar shouted: *"You are all doomed! Ashbon will kill you and rip your pitiful carcasses to shreds! None of you will survive!"*

The Posse backed away, the defiant man still in a rage, yelling and shaking his fists at his opponents, his screams of defiance suddenly turning into a moment of frantic horror, Bondar attacking without warning. Grabbing at his leg, Logar's hand grew warm from the stream of blood shooting out of his femoral artery, his leg gone. Two Stars then hit him hard in his midsection, driving his worthless carcass to the bottom and slamming it into a depression in the jagged reef. Logar's eyes remained wide open, his face frozen in evil distortion, air from his final breath lazily drifting to the surface, signaling his demise.

Witnessing the ferocious assault, Socrates waited for a few moments before engaging the hammerheads: "You two, uh, okay? I thought for a moment you were going to finish him off by eating him."

Two Stars reply was cold; "It's like what Kooks said, the Macho Blancos' response after tearing Monegore apart: "We do not eat … *slime!*"

Bondar, still in a rage with blood from the attack swirling through his teeth, adding; "You saw what he did to Schooner and his little friend! Justice only succeeds against this kind of evil when met with swift response! If allowed to linger, it rapidly spreads! Oh, by the way, not one word to Peetie. He does not need to know about this."

Socrates had nothing to say in response, just nodding his head and swimming away to rejoin the Posse.

Malanai then urged Tooney: "Follow me; we have to take care of your wound."

Hurrying to shore, the Posse dismounted, Sam gathering Tooney in his arms and laying him in some soft grass before removing his shirt and ripping it into long strips with the aid of his divers knife and making a tourniquet for stopping the moderate flow of blood from the gash on top of Tooneys leg.

Malanai quickly grabbed some leafy branches from a nearby ground cover and took off running toward a fresh water stream flowing adjacent to the base of the tower. Locating a small pool along its bank, she dipped the leaves in the water, shaking them violently. The action created a soapy froth into which she dipped her head, scrubbing her beautiful long hair and rinsing it several times before yanking several strands from her scalp, weaving three of them into a thin braid using two curved fragments of bone she kept looped in a belt worn around her waist. Running back to Tooneys side, she frantically implored Sam; "I need a small sharp object to help stitch the wound!" Sam quickly reached for a sealed neoprene pouch he kept strapped to his waist. Inside the emergency kit was exactly what Malanai was looking for: a sewing needle. Plucking it out of Sam's hand and running back to the pool, she began scrubbing the curled inside surface of a palm frond base and filling the shallow basin with the water, after which she dropped the needle inside. Upon returning, she requested Sam and Ben to hold Tooney down and for Chloe to hold his hands and keep him talking. Malanai then slowly poured some of the sterilized water directly over the open wound, using the three-strand braid of woven hair and the needle to administer necessary stitches. Surprisingly, Tooney did not so as much as flinch during the procedure, saying to Chloe,

"Pain is only a perception: what you cannot see, you usually do not feel."

Nodding her head in agreement she responded; "I will definitely try to remember that, Tooney." Then rolling her eyes and whispering to her dad out of the corner of her mouth she comically asked; "He didn't, uh, happen to *drink* any of that soapy water, did he?"

Grabbing one of the remaining pieces of Sam's shirt, Malanai dipped it in the water, finishing the emergency aid by applying a protective wrap and instructing Sam; "Go to the top of the stream where the current is strong. Find a fallen palm frond, cut off the leafy stalk and scrub its curled base before filling it with clear water. Have Tooney drink as much as he can; he has lost a lot of blood. I have got to help the dolphin now."

Malanai grabbed what was left of Sam's shirt, ripping it with his knife into long thin pieces and rinsing them in the balance of the frothy water before sprinting out into the sea. The only problem was that Schooner was too far away from the shoreline for Malanai to help him. Chloe saw her dilemma and, gently stroking Tooneys hand, said to him; "Tooney, I have to help Malanai with your dolphin. Are you okay? I need to go ... *right now!*"

The young man nodded and Chloe sped away, knowing exactly what to do. Reaching waist deep water she began slapping her hands hard on the surface, Schooner responding in a heartbeat. Chloe carefully caressed the beautiful creature while Malanai tended to his fin. The cut was not too deep. Therefore, after treating the area with the natural sterilant, there was no need for stitching it up. However, pulling the fin back just enough to close the flesh she looped a strip of fabric around the top front-side of the fin and a slight depression in its rear base, pulling tight and securing the compress with a knot to keep the wound closed. She and Chloe then eased the young dolphin back into deeper water. Schooner did not want them to leave his side, staying close and chirping his appreciation while twitching his head up and down. Chloe and Malanai responded by gently stroking his face and kissing him on his snout.

Once back on shore, Malanai urged the Posse to settle in and take a breather while she joined Ben in searching out a food source. Socrates and his friends took off following Amaya, Serine, and Zippee, the trio having located a wide channel beneath a curvature in the cliff-face several hundred feet away from the temple tower.

Chapter 21

A cold chill ran up Joleen's spine the second she began boarding the battleship USS Courier. Its sleek lines, coupled with an array of visible weaponry, betrayed its one and only purpose: to eliminate opposition. On the way up the gangplank, Nathan whispered to Joleen; "By the way Princess, the Admiral does not know that you are our daughter. Your mother and I are the Batistes'."

Joleen caught on, a smile of confidence sweeping across her face.

Admiral McCauley was excited, standing proud while awaiting the arrival of his guests. Extending his hand in greeting, he welcomed them; "Ah, Nathan and Cheyenne, welcome aboard ... once again. Who do you have tagging along?"

"Admiral McCauley, allow me to introduce you to Charlie and Carlynn Castleberry, as well as the director of our multi-tribal research association, Ms. Joleen Teal."

The Admiral was quick to greet Charlie and Carlynn. However, when Joleen stepped forward he almost passed out, her beauty completely off the charts. The crew of the battleship was looking on, Joleen's vivid blue eyes, coupled with her jet-black hair, putting them in a semi-trance. Fumbling for words from staring into her eyes the Admiral finally managed; "Ms. Teal, it is an honor to have you aboard our ship. Please, join me: I will give you a tour."

Joleen, her parents, and Charlie and Carlynn listened intently to every word of the description of the vessel, as well as its weapons capacity. It was indeed an incredible ship, yet did not possess the stealth capacity, or speed, or maneuverability of Nations Pride. Toward the end of the tour the Admiral offered; "Why don't we sit out on the deck. The breeze is nice and I have a few questions about your island's research. Would you mind, Ms. Teal?"

Graciously, Joleen replied, "Not at all, Admiral; I would welcome the interchange."

Once seated, the Admiral got right to the point: "Ms. Teal, it appears that something strange is occurring in the Triangle that demands an explanation."

Playing along Joleen asked; "What explicitly are your referring to Admiral?"

"Well, two United States warships recently took down a large vessel which had been commandeered two years ago by Pirates off the Somali coast and modified for their criminal activities. The pirate Captain, who is now in custody, is railing over someone attacking his ship without warning in international waters. He is claiming that an intense beam of light coming from the Earth's outer atmosphere set his vessel ablaze, causing his entire crew to abandon ship. That all evidently happened just prior to our F16s sinking his vessel. Both commanders of our warships testified that, for a moment, they did witness a bright flash, yet by the time our Fl6s responded no such light was in evidence. They also mentioned receiving a covert message from one … Seal Team Six. What I am personally curious about is; what Seal Team Six are we talking about? Moreover, what sort of luminary could possibly cause such a ghostly conflagration?"

The Admiral suddenly shifted his eyes over to Charlie and Carlynn: "You two were spotted on camera alongside Ms.

Teal aboard the Ocean Gem within a couple of weeks after returning to Port. I assume you are Tooneys parents, right? Tell me, how is the boy and Captain Sam O'Brien. Surely, they must be nearby. I am curious about Captain O'Brien's request for help with a map."

The air grew thick from the Admiral's probing, yet Joleen knew how to put a stop to it: "Why of course, the mapping for our research. It has to do with employing a new technology. Perhaps you could help us by locating some Russian and Japanese fishing trawlers north of Antarctica. We have research to share with them that could possibly curb their illegal activity, giving them ample reason to take a more sustainable approach to our planet's resources. You wouldn't happen to have any coordinates to share with us regarding their whereabouts, would you?"

The Admiral was visibly perturbed at Joleen's trumping his curiosity by making a request of her own. He looked into her eyes with a calloused stare, Joleen folding her hands, patiently awaiting his reply with a quirky smile on her face.

The Admiral responded, "Okay, I can do that for you. However, once I give you the coordinates, are you prepared to reciprocate? Look, Ms. Teal, I am not here to challenge you or interrupt your research. I am here to help. The United

States War Department is demanding answers and I am your best bet for running interference. The military is currently targeting your island in a search for answers, as I am sure you are well aware. I believe you recently incurred a visit by some other... military vessels. It amazes me the goose chase they encountered once they entered these waters. It seems as though a Clingon Warship was involved. You, uh, wouldn't know anything about that, would you?"

Instantly, Charlie coughed, covering his mouth from a chuckle, saying, "Oh, excuse me Admiral. This breeze seems to be drying out my throat. You wouldn't mind fetching me something to drink, would you?"

The Admiral smiled, knowing that Charlie's cough was more of a muffled burst of laughter. Snapping his fingers, a young sailor responded by getting a pitcher of water and several glasses.

McCauley's suppositions were spot on, yet Joleen was not intimidated by his cold nature. After a few tense moments, Joleen offered; "Okay Admiral, we accept your offer. Only, I am curious as to why the Military would be interested in, among other things, isopod exploration, as well as the proliferation of ocean species. However, if you can help us by securing an extended boundary for our Native American research, perhaps we can share some of what we have learned. After all, we are committed to helping humankind and the technology we are developing will be a step in the right direction, if placed in the hands of someone with integrity. Just a word of caution though; the Sovereign waters your government feels it can enter without proper authorization do have a level of protection that, believe me, you are in no way prepared to deal with."

The Admiral's eyes were aflame from Joleen's threat, the young woman appearing aloof and cold hearted. Nathan interrupted for a moment; "Admiral, you should keep in mind that *you* are the guest here. I know Ms. Teal and she is not trying to be confrontational, only practical. What she is offering is a fair trade. I suggest you take her up on it. I have never known her to go back on her word. Besides, what harm can it do to extend a research boundary in the midst of a hard to navigate, uninhabitable, ocean wilderness?"

The Admiral stood up, angrily pushing his chair out of the way and folding his arms, turning away and pacing back and forth across the deck, all the while seething at Joleen's offer, feeling that she knew what she would be getting out of the agreement but not knowing exactly what he could expect. Reading him like a book, Joleen concluded, "Don't worry

Admiral: we are a civilized people. What we offer will never put *you* on a ...*Trail of Tears*. Do we have an agreement?"

His irritated reply; "Yes, young lady, we have an agreement!" He then called for the officer in charge of navigation to expedite the location of Japanese and Russian fishing and whaling ships operating in the South Pacific. Locating a five-ship fleet of Japanese fishing vessels, the navigational team determined that protesters using water cannons were trying to deter their progress. The Admiral invited Joleen and her entourage onto the command deck to see the images: "There, is that what you are looking for? You can see from this satellite feed that the usual protests are taking place. Boy, I wish there were some way to stop those unconscionable jerks from destroying every creature in their path. I sure hope you can help. If it were up to me our fleet would simply eliminate the offenders. However, with our resources stretched to the limit worldwide, we cannot afford sparking an international incident."

Joleen replied, "Don't worry Admiral; this is right up our alley." Then leaning over she whispered to him, "Regardless of what happens; no chatter ... understood?"

Admiral McCauley suddenly felt a tinge of trust sweep over him, realizing that this amazing woman had her world in total control. He admired the fact that she would not back down, a person uniquely possessing the required grit to oversee people as well as resources. For some unknown reason, in spite of his internal battle with his own stubborn nature, he liked her. Concluding the meeting, Joleen held out her hand, the Admiral clasping it in both of his and concluding; "Ms. Teal, it will be a pleasure working with you."

"I, too, am looking forward to it, Admiral. Perhaps you would be interested in a video tour of our aquatic research. I can have it downloaded and sent over say, by morning. I am sure your crew will enjoy the presentation."

The Admiral's eyes narrowed, thinking he was going to get a guided excursion to the island. Instead, Joleen was offering a … video tour. He gave her a look as though to say, "What are you up to young lady?"

Nathan and Cheyenne, as well as Charlie and Carlynn, concluded with their own farewell pleasantries, Joleen covertly slipping out her phone and taking a snapshot of the satellite feed of the Japanese trawlers while the Admirals back was turned. She then stepped forward: "Our tour of your ship has been very educational Admiral."

Handing her a printed copy of the current location of the Japanese fishing fleet, he replied; "I do hope this helps."

Chapter 22

Arriving back on the island, Charlie and Carlynn joined Corey to perform a systems check aboard Nations Pride. After escorting her parents to the new technologies lab, Joleen proceeded with instructions to her staff on island security procedures. She then requested James and Joseph to assist her, the trio hurrying to join their crew aboard the ship. Upon arrival, Corey greeted them by clasping his hands together, stretching out his arms and reversing his wrists causing his fingers to crack. Joleen shivered; "I wish you wouldn't do that. It gives me chills."

"I am sorry Ms. Teal; it is a nervous habit. I always do it when I get excited. My assumption is that we are going to be up to some mischief today?"

Handing Corey her phone and the printout the Admiral had given her she said; "Here, download my last photo and these detailed coordinates into the ships computer. I will wait here with my parents while the rest of you get Nations Pride back out to sea. Head due east, getting about fifty miles off our coast before launching the Raptor. Fly the bird east around the globe; I want the approach to Antarctica from the west. Charlie, you and James will have to determine which fishing vessel the protesters are targeting. That will be the ship running interference for the rest of the fleet. Light that vessel up and get the Raptor out of there on a heading due north. We can only hope the crew abandons ship. Allow five minutes before returning and … rotate the carriage."

Charlie's eyes opened wide, asking, "Are we going to … like … make it go---*poof*?"

"Yes Charlie, we are going to … like … make it go---*poof.*"

Standing alongside Charlie with his arms folded across his chest, Joseph Hawks' face broke into a huge grin, saying, "Mmmm, good idea."

Joleen continued, "Okay, get the ship ready before taking some time to rest. We strike at midnight, which means you need to be out of here by 10:30 p.m. The weather reports from halfway around the world show the sun shining brightly north of Antarctica around noon their time." Then, hesitating for a moment before leaving the ship, an air of defiance began molding her face: "Friends ... our battle begins."

Nations Pride submerged exactly on time, heading out of its subterranean nest and into the open ocean. Corey and crew followed Ms. Teal's directions to the letter, achieving their proper separation from the island within an hour. Charlie then began communicating signals to the Raptor's launching pad, a camouflaged roof sliding out of position allowing for the aircraft's vertical take-off and almost instantaneous disappearance into the upper atmosphere, its speed ramping-up to mach 30. It took only twenty-three minutes for the Raptor to reach its destination, Charlie timing the strike to the second. Just as the satellite imagery projected aboard the USS Courier, protesters were still engaged with a vessel specially equipped for dealing with those opposed to their so-called research. Water cannons were blasting away from both ships, inundating their crews and equipment. However, in an instant, that activity stopped, light from the Raptor's laser infusing every molecule of the Japanese vessel, the fiery conflagration of phantom light causing the ship's crew to scream in panic while leaping into the sea. The protestors were also scared out of their wits, the intense light blinding their vision. The Raptor then sped away, Charlie sending a signal for carriage rotation. Moments later, while the protestors were busy rescuing the Japanese sailors, the Raptor returned, Charlie refocusing on the target vessel, and in an instant---*POOF*; the entire ship disappeared into thin air. James then uploaded an image into an orbiting satellite over the location of the incident while Charlie was busy getting the Raptor back to home base.

Just after midnight, aboard the USS Courier, Admiral McCauley was awakening to the sound of someone banging on the door of his quarters: *"WHAT IS IT?"* he shouted.

"Admiral, come quick sir; the commander is demanding your presence in the control center!"

The Admiral quickly dressed and sprinted to the helm, the ship's Commander waving his arms for him to hurry. Once in the control center, the commander directed the Admiral's attention to a secure, real-time monitor and asked; "What do you make of this, Sir?"

The live feed from a military satellite, some halfway around the globe, was displaying images from coordinates the Admiral previously shared with Joleen, the crew of the protest ship busy rescuing people from the frigid water near Antarctica, survivors no doubt of the ship running interference for the

Japanese fishing fleet. The Admiral asked, "What happened to the opposing ship?"

The Lieutenant in charge of communications answered, "We do not know, Sir. It seemingly vanished into … thin air."

The Admiral stared hard at the screen, the thought of a ship vanishing making no sense. However, the Lieutenant shouted out, "Wait; we are downloading more images from a Japanese satellite that passed over the area within the last couple of hours. What in the world---?"

The satellite imagery projected a stream of intense light coming from the sky, its powerful rays turning the ship into a fireball. The feed from the satellite also revealed its source, the Commander commenting with a chuckle in his voice; "Admiral, meet the perpetrator. If my memory serves me right, I think that is … Godzilla."

Admiral McCauley's face was stern, yet he could not contain his urge to laugh, knowing that somehow Ms. Teal had to be involved, and her previous request for these very coordinates certainly having a purpose. Addressing the ship's commander, Admiral McCauley stated, "Have your men stand down. I am sure an explanation will be forthcoming in the morning."

The following morning Joleen decided to pay another visit to the Admiral, this time taking along Molly and Bonnie Mae, all three arriving barefoot and dressed in traditional beaded buckskin dresses. Upon boarding the USS Courier, Joleen handed the Admiral a CD featuring their island's efforts to understand nautical environments, including recently dubbed in sperm whale codas. Joleen offered; "Admiral, my two assistants and I would appreciate the opportunity to bring you and your crew up to date on some of our research."

"Nothing would please us more Ms. Teal. Your island's accomplishments are starting to raise many questions. I am sure a personal narration of your video production will take the edge off common suspicions, as well as relieve the crew's boredom. Perhaps we can follow it up with some Japanese Sci-Fi. I understand some of their nation's fishermen recently had a run in with ... Godzilla."

Controlling her urge to laugh, Joleen responded, "Why, Admiral, that would be a welcome treat. I have been wondering when Japanese producers were going to get around to resurrecting that wily old monster. He seemed to have a habit of showing up ... unexpected."

The Admiral's eyes narrowed; "Yes he did, Ms. Teal, he certainly did."

The starry-eyed crew began gathering quickly, the ship's commander having arranged a rotating schedule. The officers were the first of three groups to be entertained by the thirty-minute production. Joleen began the narration with a ten-minute video reminder of the past two-hundred years of Native North American tribal history and the indignities suffered by indigenous people as a result of having their homelands forcefully taken away and subsequently occupied by European settlers, the oration leaving each sailor misty eyed. Turning the microphone over to Molly and Bonnie Mae, the duo took turns explaining the successes of their island's aquatic research and earth friendly resource development. Ending the presentation with a chorus of sperm whale codas left the commander and crew dumbfounded, the clarity of the songs surpassing any previous attempt to capture nature's most unique audible, the decibel level higher than that of any other creature on the planet. In conclusion, Joleen stated; "Gentlemen and ladies, it is a unique privilege to share our accomplishments with you. We wish to leave each of you a token gift, an expression of our love for our research and our hope for future generations. Perhaps its message will inspire each of you with your own, personal endeavors."

Molly and Bonnie Mae then presented each individual with a poster featuring their island logo of a majestic golden eagle in flight grasping a beautifully colored world globe, the words beneath it reading---'One world, clutched in the talons of wisdom'. The effect of the poster made a deep impression on the sailors, all sharing in thunderous applause while expressing gratitude for the effort the island residents were making toward forging a better future through cultural understanding and nature research.

When the presentation concluded, the Admiral turned away and walked over to the coffee machine while dabbing his teary eyes with a handkerchief. His mind began drifting back to the days when he and Sam O'Brien tried so hard to get the Federal Government to extend funding for their isopod research. He reluctantly caved in to the urgings of the military, accepting their offer as an advisor instead of pursuing his dream of exploring aquatic sciences in the private sector. Ms. Teals' accomplishments were exactly what he hoped to achieve when he was a young man.

Strolling over to the Admiral's side, Joleen whispered to him, "Now, about your offer of a glimpse into Godzilla's new episode; does that offer still hold?"

The Admiral had just taken a swallow of coffee when an unexpected chuckle caused a geyser to erupt from his mouth and nose, Joleen quickly responding with a paper towel. Upon recovering from the embarrassing reaction to her request, he smiled; "Ms. Teal, it would be my pleasure to treat you to that rascal's latest episode."

The video of the previous night's incident brought a mischievous smile to Joleen's' face, Molly and Bonnie Mae covering their mouths, huddling up and snickering. Joleen then commented; "Wow, those producers certainly have their video effects near perfection these days. I am certain that any fishing fleet is certainly going to think twice about engaging in any future activity that negatively impacts that big boy's world." Turning to the Admiral, she asked, "So, what we are seeing is a recent release, is it?"

Admiral McCauley exhaled a deep sigh; "Yes, Ms. Teal, a very recent release."

Escorting Joleen and her young associates to the ship's exit ramp, the Admiral took her hand in his, thanking her for taking the time to educate his crew on the work her island residents were engaging in. Joleen smiled; "Why, thank you Admiral. I am comforted by your crew's response. With so much uncertainty gripping our world, I feel it pays to share the things that really count. Perhaps you will have an opportunity to share in our next adventure. Good day, Admiral."

Keeping eye contact, he turned his head slightly sideways, responding, "What adventure are you specifically referring to … Ms. Teal?"

"Later, Admiral; we will talk about it later."

Chapter 23

Leaning against a post on the pier, with a smile on his face and his hands in his pockets, Corey was hamming it up, singing a legendary soundtrack from the nineteen-sixties entitled, 'Catch us if you can'. He actually surprised Molly and Bonnie Mae, his voice remarkably good. After finishing the song he stretched his arms out wide, took a deep breath and said, "Oh yeah, it feels good to cut the opposition down to size."

Charlie then poked his head out of the hatch, asking Joleen, "Seen any good monster movies lately?"

She replied; "Oh, you mean like King Kong or perhaps … *Godzilla*. By the way, you kept our ship out a little late. I did not see it docked when we left this morning?"

Charlie froze for a moment, giving Joleen a curious stare; "How did you find out about Godzilla?"

"Well, the girls and I took a little excursion of our own this morning, back to the Admiral's ship, trying our best to create a diversion for you. After we concluded our presentation of our island's research, the Admiral treated us to a film clip of one of Godzilla's latest episodes. So, Charlie, are you happy with your new creation?"

"Lady, I am very happy. I feel better than I have in years. Our new toy gives a whole new meaning to the word, 'Poof'. However, this is no time to rest. I suggest we get busy planning our next mission."

Squinting her eyes, she asked him, "What do you happen to have in mind, Sir?"

Charlie gave Corey a nod, an indication to come back on board to show Ms. Teal his new discovery. Joleen and the girls climbed onboard, following Corey to his control panel. With the click of a mouse, a three dimensional graphic appeared on screen linking the golden cavern, where Sam and the others disappeared, with the deep trench the sperm whales previously guided them to, including the exact location of the quivering corridor they broadcasted their Morse code message through. Corey explained; "We revisited the deep water trench last night. Remember our discussion some days ago about a guesstimated separation between caverns of two and one-half miles and their elliptical arrangement allowing for unlimited growth?"

Joleen nodded her head in the affirmative, her voice stretching her reply, "Yes, yes I remember."

"Well, we re-mapped the walls of the surrounding area. I mentioned before that they looked as if someone chiseled them out by hand. A closer look revealed that the abrupt wall behind our ship, while we were facing the anomaly, is perfectly perpendicular to the laser-straight walls on our port and starboard sides. What we have discovered is literally an oceanic box canyon. Watch what happens when I draw a line from the center of the wall behind us, keeping its vector perfectly parallel to the walls on either side of our ship, yet angling it upward from our depth of four thousand five hundred feet to sea level. It lands us dead center over the middle of the canyon containing the giant crystal, some seven hundred and twenty miles away. Now, we are going to extend this line through the canyon and mark a spot exactly two and one-half miles on the other side of its perimeter. We will call the spot, GE. Starting on this mark, we draw an elliptical circle to the east, using a 23.45-degree arc, the same degree as the tilt of the earth on its axis. We are going to mark an additional spot on this arc every two and one half miles.

Interestingly, the second mark on this trajectory, which is five miles from GE, puts us at the exact location of the cavern where Sam and the others disappeared. I do not think this to be a coincidence. My hypothesis is that GE is, or at least was, the Grand Entry to the City of Atlantis. The only way we will ever know is to go back and check it out."

Joleen was quick to respond, "Young man, even if your theory is correct, we are going to concentrate on finding our lost friends ... *first!*"

"I understand, Ms Teal; I am not suggesting we sidetrack their rescue. Nevertheless, if you were trying to get the Admiral to secure an addition to your research boundary, I would propose the inclusion of this entire area. It would look something like---." Drawing a large rectangle, one-thousand miles long and five-hundred miles wide, which included the existing boundary of only ten thousand square miles, he explained: "I know it looks like an extraordinarily large area. However, it is aquatic wilderness, having no real value except for established shipping lanes, which you could use for the purpose of compromise. That is, if you agree to allow ship traffic through without shooting arrows at them for criminal trespass."

Ms. Teal took a moment, strolling back and forth, thinking of how Corey's suggestion might affect their attempt at a rescue while keeping the Admiral's involvement to a minimum. James suddenly broke the silence; "Joleen, I think Corey is on to something. Look at the advantage we have. If we run into a problem, we use our Raptor, which means we will have the freedom to move around aboard ship, not hampered by all those bulky quivers filled with arrows. The man is a genius."

Joleen sighed, while the rest of the crew bent over in laughter. However, their light-hearted moment quickly subsided, interrupted by an abrupt banging on the hatch, a voice shouting: *"Ms. Teal, come quickly!"*

The voice was that of Johnny Tairell, one of the young scouts assigned to Joleen's tender to the battleships: "Ms. Teal, one of the ships is pulling away. Our scouts just alerted us that the Admiral is claiming an emergency. Please, maam, we need to *hurry!*"

Joleen instantly barked out orders; "James, you come with me! Charlie, you and Carlynn get aboard Nations Pride and make sure the Raptor is prepared to fly. Corey, get this ship ready for launch within the hour! Molly and Bonnie Mae, we are going to need your help. Change your clothes and report back here, ASAP! Joseph, go to our command center; the island is to stay on high alert. Have my parents help in any way you see fit. Make sure all communication with our island stays shut down until we can determine what is happening. This could be it people; I have a feeling our battle is ramping up."

Joleen, James, and Johnny Tairell sprinted away in a dead heat, hoping the USS Courier was still holding its position off their island's coast. Joleen breathed a sigh of relief once clearing the outreaches of the cove and spotting the ship. The Admiral, anxiously watching and waiting on the bow, began waving his arms, urging the small craft to hurry. Lowering the gangplank, several of the ships' crewmembers helped Joleen and James aboard. The Admiral was quick to engage; "Ms. Teal, we were just notified from Atlantic fleet command that another ship from the African coast has entered the same area where our military took down the pirate vessel. Our best guess is that it is a sister ship. Headquarters issued us an order to intercept only moments ago. Our return to your island is a bit uncertain in the short term. Do you have any requests before we leave your tribal waters?"

"Actually, I have something of great importance to share with you Admiral. Can we have a moment with you in your command center?"

"Yes Maam."

Once in the command center, Joleen asked one of the crewmembers for a digital display of the entire Atlantic Ocean. Joleen's eyes just about popped out of her head when a detailed map came up on the command center's incident screen, complete with three-dimensional sea floor topography. However, she quickly took a cursor and began drawing a huge parallelogram marking a definitive boundary for the expansion of their Sovereign tribal waters: "Admiral, our tribes are hereby claiming this entire region of the Atlantic for a marine preserve."

The Admiral looked perplexed; "Ms. Teal, that boundary is a large chunk of ocean. It would take an act of congress, as well as international treaties, to accommodate such a request."

Joleen looked him in the eyes and said, "The U.S. Congress is as impotent as a dead sea slug. In addition, I personally do not care about hollow international treaties. I am hereby *claiming* these waters for our research. You said you wanted to help. Believe me; this boundary will prove to be just as much in your interest as it is in ours. Normal shipping lanes can continue open; however, you, Admiral, will be our point of contact for any other reasonable request for access. Put the world on notice, Sir, that from this day forward the Native North American tribes are *staking their claim* to everything within this boundary for their research. You, of all people, should know it does not need to be too hard for the world to accept our declaration, most nations seemingly pleased to turn over the dregs of the planet to those they consider ... *undesirable.*"

The Admiral stood dumbfounded, his head nodding up and down and sideways, not really knowing how to respond. He finally stated; "You got it, Princess. We will make the declaration and do everything in our power to establish it as legally binding. For now though, would you like to tag along? It looks as though we will be prosecuting our ship's first case of criminal trespass within your border."

Joleen smiled; "Why thank you, Admiral. However, James and I will have to take a rain check on your offer, for today at least. We are content with our own mode of transportation. Good day."

After leaving the ship, James asked Joleen, "What did you just do? Do you think governments of the world are going to roll over and accept a declaration of an addition to your sovereign territory without any dialog? You are setting yourself up for *war!*"

Joleen's hair was blowing in the wind while standing next to Johnny Tairell at the center console, her eyes wild with wonder, her face donning a smile from ear to ear; "Yes, I know. However, any challenge we might face in battle will immediately result in shrinking the opposition's forces. If we are careful, the only harm we stand to impose will be to any offenders' assets, not to human personnel." She then turned around, throwing her arms around James' neck, giving him a big hug and re-assuring him; "This is a fight we will not lose. Our future hinges on our success and we *will stand* for what we *know* is right. We have reached that threshold cousin when it is time to ... *paint our faces!*"

Chapter 24

Joleen was not kidding. As soon as their boat arrived at the dock, she hurried Johnny and James to the ceremonial grounds. From there she sent the island residents a rallying signal on a set of Tom-Tom's. The response was quick, the beat … a clear indication of war. Each team took their station, patiently awaiting instructions. Joleen stood facing the diverse groups of tribal representatives, her face already painted with a single red line from the top of her forehead to the tip of her nose, coupled with three stripes swiped diagonally across both cheeks of her face. Her hair was pulled back, being held fast with a headband, its white background emblazoned across the front with a blood-red Comanche arrow. Her short narrative got right to the point: "We knew this day would come. Our research has cast us into a situation that demands taking a stand to preserve what we have accomplished for the good of our planet. Nothing we do from here on out will be viewed as popular by any of the world's nations. Today we made a declaration aboard a United States battleship laying claim to an expansion of our tribal aquatic territory … including our find of the ancient city of Atlantis. We are already facing our first challenge, an enemy trespasser closing in on the coordinates to the cavern where our friends disappeared. The United States Military is right now speeding to intercept. From this moment, Johnny Tairell will manage all communication on this island. He will coordinate the runners as well as the drummers. Nations Pride will launch shortly, sizing up our opposition and hopefully using the Navy's resources as a diversion. James and I will need a quick word with each team leader. My friends, we have reached that day when we *paint our faces!* Whatever direction this battle takes, be assured; *we will succeed!* This is the day we begin teaching all nations of the world that they cannot take what is not theirs without consequences! They will learn that trifling with this planet's resources and exploiting them for selfish gain will result in our meting out justice speedily. *Never again will anyone steal our accomplishments, displace our people, or trample on our heritage! Today we stand in the moccasins of our ancestors and turn their demise back into legend! Their legacy of pride will once again live and become a beacon of hope for all who love this beautiful planet! Will you stand with me?"*

The response to Joleen's appeal was deafening, each tribe shouting affirmation to the declaration in its own native language. The beat on the Tom-Toms began instantly, inciting the lighting of a ceremonial fire. Huge containers of paint drained quickly as each resident colored his or her face with tribal markings for battle. Joleen rallied the leaders, giving each detailed instructions for protecting the island before participating in the dances, the pulsating rhythm building to a fever pitch before erupting into a unified war cry. An eerie hush quickly followed, the entire assembly dispersing to their respective assignments.

Joseph Hawk stood his ground, awaiting instructions with Joleen's parents. Nathan and Cheyenne were feeling proud of the command their daughter exhibited, the island residents not questioning a word. What they saw was not people responding out of blind faith; rather, the reaction was one of trust, respect, and love for their leader. Joleen gave not a soul reason to doubt her strategy. Her confidence in the tribes' abilities made everyone feel they were a necessary part of the island's purpose. Nathan wanted to hug her; however, this was no time for sentiment. Standing next to Joseph, he took his wife's hand awaiting instructions.

Joleen was decisive and to the point: "Joseph, take my folks with you to the war terminal. Have them help you with checking our provision centers and safe rooms beneath the lodges. Make sure all air passages and water conduits are unobstructed in case there is an incident forcing you to take cover. I want every detail covered like clockwork. James and I are taking Charlie and Carlynn with us, along with Molly and Bonnie Mae. See to it that the New Technologies team stays alert. We are going to need the Raptor shortly. It will probably be running multiple sorties before this is over so, each time it returns, ready it again as fast as you possibly can."

Joleen then leaned forward, giving Joseph a hug and a peck on his cheek. Then, looking her parents in the eyes said; "This is what you trained me for. Your spirit will always live in my heart."

She then took off running, hurrying up the trail with her team to board Nations Pride.

Molly and Bonnie Mae cast the dock lines into the water, the ship immediately submerging. Once clearing the subterranean canal, Corey broadcast the audio of the sperm whale codas as well as the humpback's solitary song. Surprisingly, Big Jake was only a mile off the coast, apparently awaiting their ships return to sea. Corey enhanced the video of everything within reach of his monitors only to see at least fifty sperm whales fall in position behind the big humpback and join in following the ship. Joleen stood near the helm with Molly and Bonnie Mae, the trio fascinated by the mammals' curiosity.

Corey swallowed hard, whispering under his breath, "Sorry big fellah, but we are in a hurry." He then accelerated to seventy knots, a speed too fast for the mammals to keep up. All Corey could hope for was that the big humpback could sense they were heading back to the cavern where Sam and the others disappeared. For the moment that did not matter. Getting to the site before the battleships arrived was of primary importance.

Eight hours passed before Joleen entered the Raptors' control room, addressing Charlie, "Are we in a position to beat the battleships to our mark?"

"Yes maam, we are. Our current calculations show us arriving approximately thirty-seven minutes before the lead ship. We will be approaching the outer rim of the caverns shortly. May I add a little icing to our cake?"

Joleen gave Charlie a look and a grin, asking, "What are you up to now, mister?"

"Oh, just a little something I forgot to tell you about. While we were working on the Raptor, I remembered something Buddy said about seascape imagery. So, I decided it would be nice to incorporate his idea into something that would enhance our Raptor's ability." Pulling up an image on his personal computer tablet, he explained; "Notice, just under the nose of our aircraft you will see a dark, five inch oval lens. We were able to fit a military grade, high def camera into the nose of our bird, giving us the ability to see a white footed ant on a palm frond in Hawaii from the outer reaches of our planet's atmosphere. I thought it would be a nice touch, just in case we need it to observe our targets more closely before we … you know … we make them go---POOF."

Grabbing Charlie by the sides of his face, Joleen proceeded to lay a big kiss on his forehead; "Mister, you are a genius. How soon can we zoom in on our trespassers?"

"Well, if we launch now I would say … five minutes."

"Let's do it. Look for anything onboard that ship that appears out of the ordinary."

"You got it."

Charlie asked Joleen to bring Molly and Bonnie Mae into the room. Joleen was curious as to why, yet complied with his request. As soon as the two young maidens stepped in, Charlie explained; "While we were working on our idea for the camera, these two young ladies came up with the idea for its location. They were also the ones who performed all its pre-flight tests. So I feel it only appropriate to give them the opportunity to be the first to try it out in real time." Charlie and James then stood up, Charlie offering; "Ladies, may we offer you our seats at the console. We are interested in what you can do."

The two young women were excited and determined, quickly taking their seats and reviewing pre-flight data. Molly then requested that Corey bring them to within six fathoms of the surface. Upon reaching that mark the Raptor was airborne within only a minute, heading into the upper atmosphere before leveling off on a vector to intercept their trespassers. Molly took control of the flight pattern while Bonnie Mae handled the camera. Only moments later Molly began counting down; "five, four, three, two, and one.

Bonnie Mae then communicated with the raptor and an image on the deck of the ship came into view. With a slight touch on the monitor, the camera on the Raptor went into auto focus, making everything aboard the vessel as clear as the screen at a movie theater. It took only three or four seconds for the 'something unusual' to show up."

James blurted out, "Capture that image."

What they were seeing was a training facility, an obstacle course with dark clad fighters running through at full speed, their weapons draped across their backs. One individual in a turban was apparently shouting instructions to the combatants. Bonnie Mae positioned the camera, firing off at least a hundred images in only seconds. James shut the sortie down quickly; "Okay, girls, let's get our bird back to home base."

The girls completed their task with amazing precision, their first run a complete success. James now retook his seat, sending a signal via satellite to the Battleship USS Courier. Admiral McCauley was dumbfounded, wondering where in the world the images were coming from. However, a message following the images was crystal-clear: "Run these through your military database. Apparently our trespassers have an Isis training facility onboard. If we are not mistaken, the leader looks like the Ayatollah's son. We need answers quickly."

This time the Admiral did not question the request, knowing that somehow the phantom helper was on his side.

He began thinking of Joleen, the Choctaw Princess having preferred her own means of transport. How could anyone outmaneuver his military? The thought sent a shiver up his spine. However, his new ship had a distinct advantage when it came to its computer database. Logged in its memory was the name and photograph of every known terrorist fighter the U.S. Military was currently aware of anywhere in the world. The message was spot on. The leader was Iranian, the Ayatollah's son, while the other twenty-five fighters were all known Isis affiliates. The problem now was; how to respond to the message received. Within a couple of minutes, a second message was forthcoming; "If information is correct, have your lead ship turn hard to starboard 90 degrees. Hold course for one minute before turning 90 degrees back to port and resume course."

James kept his monitor locked onto a video feed from a military satellite, the crew aboard Nations Pride watching closely for a response. James doubled up his fist when the lead battleship listed hard to starboard before correcting its vector one minute later. Looking up at Joleen, he stated, "There are only two ways for this to go; we target only the fighters or the whole ship. If we allow any of the terrorists to go to prosecution, you know they will be back."

Joleen dropped her head, never expecting to have to make a decision about the taking of human life. Simply lighting up the vessel would be allowing the worst of the crew to survive, only to continue their spread of Islamic terrorism. Yet, if she vanquished the ship with its crew, she would be compromising her islands charter. At this point, it would be so easy to permanently deal with this situation, however---.

After a few quiet moments, Corey had an idea: "Everyone, come to the helm!"

The crew gathered quickly, wondering what Corey had in mind. Downloading a program he had been working on he looked up and said; "My friends, meet the dragon." Coming up on the screen was a three dimensional image of a thousand foot long anaconda with jaws twenty feet wide and fangs as long as football goal posts. Corey then changed the face to resemble the Ayatollah, supreme leader of Iran. The jaws of the image opened wide, its teeth dripping with slime, so seemingly life-like and real that it scared the crew. After a moment of viewing the horrifying image, he uploaded the graphic into the same military satellite, transmitting the sarcastic holographic insult directly over the trespassers, making it appear as though the Devil himself were consuming them. Screams of horror ensued, yet their fear did not stop a vain attempt to destroy the source of the heresy. An unexpected response caught the crew of Nations Pride by surprise, a sudden volley of missiles quickly launching from the deck of the ship, the heat seeking devices trying to lock on to the image's source. Unbeknownst to Corey and the crew on Nations Pride, eight F16 fighter jets had already deployed from the East Coast of the United States to confront the pirates' sister ship. Suddenly, the fighter jets split in formation, their instruments indicating target lock on five of their aircraft. Evasive maneuvers ensued, the panicky pilots trying desperately to avoid the incoming ordinance. Three of the five escaped, however, two teams ejected, not able to respond quick enough to avoid the violent intercept. The United States battleships were still too far away to confront the opposition. Joleen and the crew aboard Nations Pride felt sickened, their covert action sparking this incident. They now had no choice but to put the Raptor in the air. Molly and Bonnie Mae ran back into the control room, re-launching their bird in mere seconds. They brought the Raptor in at an altitude of only forty-seven thousand feet and, refocusing on the deck of the ship, targeted the terrorists training facility. Bonnie Mae cut the timing of the focused beam coming from the laser from four seconds to one and a half, resulting in one third of the ships interior, including personnel, to vanish. Her eyes were aflame with rage; "Let those pathetic morons deal with battling phyto-plankton for a change." Turning to the rest of the crew she asked, "What? I did not kill them. I, uh, only cut them down to the size of their IQ; is that so bad? We will leave what is left of the ship for the military to deal with!"

The crew swallowed hard, wondering what the remaining F16s were going to do. Molly re-directed the Raptor on a heading due north, getting it high in the upper atmosphere before turning it back around, making another run over the targeted ship's coordinates and taking a photo of the damage. Surprisingly, the entire ship's hull was still intact, the video feed from the Raptor revealing a massive chasm just aft of the vessels midsection. Gone were the ship's training facility, its weapons cache, as well as at least half of its propulsion systems, not to mention hundreds of thousands of gallons of fuel. The remaining crewmembers were scurrying about, their defenseless ship adrift with the remaining F16s coming in low over the horizon with weapons hot, their pilots determined to blow the vessel to kingdom come. Corey was panicking; "Oh, no, they cannot sink the ship! It is too close to the caverns and the balance of its fuel could cause an ecological disaster!"

Charlie immediately uploaded a message into a military satellite, promptly sending it to the USS Courier, the message reading: "Trespassing ship secure. Call off balance of F16s. Expedite rescue procedures for downed pilots."

Admiral McCauley was not going to take any chances, immediately calling out an order for an all hands on deck, preparing not only for a rescue, but also for necessary military action. Signaling the lead ship, it too ramped up procedures while following downloaded coordinates to the incident site. Joleen and her crew were feeling frustrated, halfway thinking they should rescue the downed pilots, yet not wanting to expose Nations Pride to the military, or anyone else. Corey suddenly shivered from a cold chill running up his spine, sensing something was amiss. He quickly began scanning the area surrounding the rogue ship, and sure enough, two Soviet submarines were trailing about twenty miles behind and speeding toward the distressed ship. Charlie immediately alerted the two U. S. battleships, hoping a major confrontation was not in the making. Joleen suddenly had an idea of her own; "Molly, get the Raptor back to home base and make it ready for another sortie. Corey, replay the codas and the humpback's song. Crank up the audio to its maximum setting. We need to arouse some help."

Corey waited for Molly to complete her task before broadcasting the blaring audio. The sound traveled amazingly fast, Corey having submerged to one hundred fathoms. The vocal reply was almost instantaneous, alerting Corey to the exact proximity of the big humpback and the trailing pod of

Sperm whales. Excitedly, he blurted out, "The codas are only ten miles out. However, I am hearing a distinct difference in the voices."

Corey cranked up the volume, training his ear on the difference in pitch and distance of the codas. Some were recognizable as coming from the pod tagging along with the big humpback. However, louder and slightly higher pitched codas were joining the chorus. His smile grew wide; "There is an additional pod responding to us." He then put his hand in the air, signaling for everyone to keep silent. The codas were becoming ever clearer, an indication the whales were honing in on their ship's location. The next few moments were tense, the Russian subs slowing in response to the volley of whale songs, their navigators fearing an unexpected impact with the behemoth creatures. Corey now got a mischievous notion, whispering under his breath; "Let's play, people." Nations Pride quickly submerged even deeper, leveling off at two hundred fathoms, Corey cranking up the audio and playing the haunting sound of the great white shark attack from the movie … 'Jaws'.

The sub commanders were now perplexed, hearing the sound of; dun, dun, dun, dun, dun, dun, dudada. The vessels cut propulsion, listening intently, trying to target the audio source. The ensuing silence was ghostly, the crews aboard the Russian subs suddenly squirming from close quarters confinement, beads of sweat starting to roll down their faces from eerie uncertainty. Corey kept changing Nations Pride's position beneath the subs and replaying the haunting sound ... dun, dun, dun, dun, dun, dun ... dudada. The overwhelming fear aboard the subs was apparently too much for some of their crew, sound waves from screams of panic reverberating through the vessels hulls. Corey began snickering over the response. He stopped the audio for a moment, waiting patiently for several minutes while gaining at least a mile's lateral distance from the vessels. He then began playing a repertoire of sperm whale codas, cranking up the volume as high as he could without blowing out his instruments. He was spending so much time playing with the sub crews that he shortly forgot all about the whales themselves. Arising out of the deep was a magnificent pod of the Piscean giants who quickly surrounded Nations Pride as if greeting an honored guest.

"What is happening," shouted Molly, "are they going to attack us?"

"Hardly," replied Joleen, "these beautiful creatures are gathering to help us."

Corey then gently propelled Nations Pride back toward the subs, slowly ascending, and leveling back off at fifty fathoms. The whales stayed close, Corey turning down the volume of the recorded codas as he neared his target. He then began rolling Nations Pride from side to side, mimicking movements of the big humpback from their last encounter. The whales joined in, swooping around both subs like children playing hide and seek, all the while singing in a constant series of clicks. Charlie came up with another idea. Putting Joleen on the com line, he cranked up the volume for an announcement to the sub Commanders, Joleen's' voice ringing out loud and clear:

"You are trespassing in Native American territorial waters! State your purpose!"

For a few moments all remained silent, the sub commanders' fear growing from their abrupt confrontation with the sperm whales coupled with a haunting female voice from the deep. Joleen waited a full two minutes before re-engaging, the sternness in her voice even more demanding:

"You are trespassing in Native American territorial waters! State your purpose!"

Suddenly, an incredible shockwave rocked the depths, followed by the emergence of another fifty sperm whales; Big

Jake had arrived, the humpback breaching multiple times on the surface in a powerful display of force. The incredible pod of female whales swarmed the subs, nudging gently up against them and forcing them down. The sub commanders were panicky and helpless, their mobility hindered by the incredible weight of the great mammals, making propulsion nearly impossible. Two torpedo tubes opened on the foreside of one sub; however, behemoth bodies were squeezing tight up against the hull, blocking the ordinance cavities. The commanders had no choice but to attempt to reverse course. All this mayhem gave Corey some breathing room, allowing him to raise Nations Pride to the six-fathom mark and relock onto a military satellite, sending a message to the USS Courier that two Russian subs are involved in the escort of the trespassing ship. The reply to his message was, "As well as two Iranian battleships."

Corey immediately pushed his yoke down, diving while turning due east, Charlie operating the scanners in order to locate the outlaw support. Sure enough, two Iranian ships were on a tear to reach the distressed subs.

Molly nudged Bonnie Mae, the two running quickly to the Raptor's control room. Corey called out, "Wait, you two; I have an idea." Reversing course, Corey headed back toward the ship they previously disabled. Replaying the audio of the big humpback caused both pods of whales to back off the subs and follow Nations Pride. Having gained several miles of separation, Corey waited, hoping beyond hope the subs would eventually surface. While waiting, Charlie decided to check all systems aboard their ship, as well as atmospheric conditions. Within only a minute he cried out, "Oh, NOOO!"

"What is it?" James asked.

"Look at the screen! Two major weather systems are converging, one from the South, the other a nor'easter! Sustained winds from both storms are already over sixty knots! They are due to slam into each other over this location within only a few hours! The forecast is for one hundred foot seas and winds up to one hundred and twenty knots! The ship adrift is doomed!"

Corey suddenly called out, "It's happening people; the subs are surfacing. Training his scanners on the subs, Corey also noticed that the Iranian battleships were slowing. Both subs emerged simultaneously, their frightened crews evacuating onto the deck like a flurry of ants responding to an intruder. The interaction of the sub and battleship crews quickly revealed their coordinated exercise. This scenario was not going to play out well with the United States military, a confrontation being inevitable. Charlie and Corey looked at each other, gulping a big dose of air, their minds stressing for ideas as to what to do. James decided it was now his turn: "Corey, turn us due south. Molly and Bonnie Mae, ready the Raptor. Joleen, clear your throat; we are going to *scare* these intruders into submission."

Corey turned Nations Pride south, all the while re-playing the codas for the sperm whales to follow, luring them out of the danger zone. After about ten miles separation, James asked Corey, "How far is the ship adrift from the caverns?"

Corey answered, "It is already within the outer boundary."

"And the subs," asked James?"

"They are closing in, Sir."

James shouted; "Molly, Bonnie Mae, get our bird in the sky!"

Once again, the Raptor streaked away from the island, quickly reaching eighty-five thousand feet and heading directly for the caverns. James filled the two young maidens in on his plan, placing his hands on their shoulders and saying, "You two can do this, just breathe easy and concentrate. This is our bird's biggest test. Let us see what we can do in a critical situation."

By now, the seas were in an angry churn, huge swells rolling across the ocean's surface at only two-second intervals. Timing was crucial for the girls' first target, Bonnie Mae at the laser's control, Molly dropping the Raptor's altitude quickly on its approach to the subs, leveling off at forty seven thousand feet. Bonnie Mae's lips were slightly quivering as she counted down ..." three, two, and one." The impact of the laser sheared four feet off the top of the first subs tower, similar to an instrument used in optical Lasik surgery resulting in shaving an outer layer of cells off the cornea of a patient's eye. It was now impossible for the vessel to submerge without filling with water. The second sub never had a chance to respond, the top of its tower also disappearing. The great swells generating from wild ocean currents were also playing havoc with the Iranian battleships, their visibility obscured by the constant up and down motion of relentless swells. Alarms were blasting away aboard the submarines, distress calls that were going unheeded because of the violent wave action. However, Bonnie Mae was not done. She targeted the decks of both battleships, the resulting impact causing the large guns gracing their decks, as well as their missile launchers, to suddenly disappear.

It was now time for the grand finale. James had Corey dive to two-hundred fathoms, and turning up the audio, he handed the mike to Joleen, her voice thundering out of the deep; *"HOW DARE YOU IGNORE MY WARNING!"*

Corey quickly pulled on the yoke, taking Nations Pride back to within six fathoms of the surface, allowing Bonnie Mae to rotate the carriage on the Raptor, getting it back aloft to sixty-five thousand feet and training her sights on the crystal in the canyon. She barely pulled it off. The focused beam no sooner energized the crystal, than a massive cloud mass rolled in, blocking the target. However, her action proved successful enough to ignite a five-mile ring of golden fire with flames erupting a thousand feet into the sky. All five trespassing vessels began spinning wildly out of control, falling prey to a massive magnetic vortex, their crews completely helpless and screaming out of morbid fear. The expansive columns of fire proved too overwhelming for the ships crews causing many to strap on their life vests and jump overboard. Corey, once again pushed down on the yoke, this time diving to only one hundred fathoms before handing Joleen the mike, her voice blaring even stronger: *"ARE YOU CHALLENGING ME? SHALL I BURN YOU ALIVE BEFORE MY GREAT WAVES CONSUME YOU?"*

Finally, a trembling voice responded to the haunting threat; *"We leave! We not want die!"*

Joleen's' response was viciously cold; *"TRESPASSING WITHIN MY BOUNDARY WILL NOT BE TOLERATED! ANY FURTHER VIOLATION WILL RESULT IN YOUR VESSELS DESTRUCTION WITHOUT WARNING! THE WATERS OF MY LAIR CAN AND WILL ... SWALLOW YOU!"*

Corey brought Nations Pride abruptly back to six fathoms, uploading one final image into a military satellite, that of a woman's face emerging out of the dark grey cloud-mass above the canyon, her eyes aflame with anger. He transmitted the video to the Iranian ships with an audio of the woman shouting out a final warning: *"LEAVE HERE, AND NEVER RETURN!"*

Only seconds later, the flames retreated and the vortex calmed. However, the major storm was gaining strength. Molly sent the Raptor back to its nest, leaving all five trespassing vessels locked in crisis, their crews incapacitated from the effects of sudden overwhelming terror. It was now time for a final message to the USS Courier: "Violators condition is critical; escort them out of these waters."

Chapter 25

The powerful drift merging from the south pushed all five vessels some thirty miles north of the caverns before the military could catch up. The lead U.S. battleship arrived in time to pluck the downed pilots as well as at least fifty of the ships survivors from the water before engaging the Russian and Iranian coalition. Fortunately, for Joleen and the crew of Nations Pride, the dozens of sperm whales, though miles away, kept vocalizing during the entire incident, indicating to the U.S. Commanders the legitimacy of Joleen's claim to these waters as a nature preserve. It was now time for Joleen and her crew to assess their next move. After some twenty or so minutes of silence Corey asked, "Ms. Teal, weather reports show this to be an excessively massive storm. Within the hour, the currents are going to make our navigation difficult, even though we remain submerged. So, what do we do next?"

Joleen was leaning on the console of the helm, her eyes shifting back and forth from consuming thoughts of further conflict. James stepped up and, putting his arm around her shoulder, offered; "Cousin, I know that what just happened is going to somehow have some serious repercussions; yet, I do have an idea."

It took a moment before Joleen closed her eyes, shook her head, and asked; "I am sorry. You said … something?"

James replied, "Yes, I have an idea. Do you want to hear it?"

Joleen's thoughts finally recovered from trying to process the ramifications of her crew's previous actions. Looking around she apologized; "I am so sorry."

Molly and Bonnie Mae nestled in beside her; "We love you Ms. Teal. Do not be frightened. Together, we will get past this."

Joleen held both girls tight for a moment before addressing James; "So, what is your plan?"

"We previously received a Morse code message just out of the mouth of the cavern where Sam and the others disappeared, a distress call from one, Anders Highley. I am thinking that if the crystal in the canyon caused the activation of the strange corridor you described, and the message we sent from the trench stating that our rescue attempt will be from the cavern where the team was lost, why not get to that cavern right now and broadcast a new message. We can only hope that the corridor briefly opened."

Joleen thought about James' proposal for a moment before asking, "And what are we supposed say, seeing that we cannot even begin to help because of this crazy storm?"

"Tell them we are reversing our strategy; we will be coming in from the direction of the trench."

Joleen fired back, "Are you *crazy*? We cannot send anyone in from that depth!"

"No, no we can't, individually. However, we at least know that the corridor is big enough for our ship to fit through."

Joleen's face was now grim, their situation dire and the logistics of the operation getting more complicated by the second. After thinking for a moment she addressed Corey; "Hurry us to the mouth of the cavern and prepare to send the message! Then turning to James she added; "Whatever your plan, get to it and don't waste any time."

James immediately began figuring out the message in Morse code while Corey fought the currents, bringing Nations Pride back to the same coordinates where they received the original mayday transmission from Anders Highley. James sent the text twenty times in fifteen-second intervals: "Conditions too perilous at this location … Will attempt rescue at site of previous transmission." He then turned to Corey and said, "Get us back to the island."

Suddenly, an incredible explosion rocked the depths, Corey quickly scanning the area for the source. His monitors finally trained on one of the Iranian ships in obvious peril. The Russian subs were flailing, engulfed in the extreme weather conditions, and unable to submerge due to the Raptors removing their towers. The sub commanders could only expect the Iranian battleships to help in their time of peril. However, their fickle escorts chose instead to turn tail and run. The Russian sub commanders responded to the betrayal by launching two volleys each of torpedoes. Two of the projectiles reached their target, blowing the stern completely off one of the battleships and igniting its entire fuel supply. The explosion was extremely violent, some of the scattered debris and hot ordinance even reaching and setting fire to the deck of the sister ship, that ship's crew scrambling to launch lifeboats amidst overwhelming heat from the flames, in addition to a constant pounding of sixty to one hundred foot swells. The topsy-turvy wave action caused the fire to spread rapidly, eventually igniting not only the ship's fuel supply, but also the balance of its massive payload of stored ordinance, the resulting explosion rivaling that of a nuclear bomb in amid one of the most horrendous storms on record. Within only minutes all semblance of the burning Iranian ships vanished, disappearing into the deep like an imploded star system into a galactic black hole. All that was left of the event was a few tattered lifeboats with survivors helplessly clinging to debris while the crippled subs were bobbing around on the surface like corks, unable to submerge. The pirate ship fared no differently, the massive cavity within its interior filling rapidly with water, forcing the balance of its crew into abandoning hope, the vessel slipping quickly beneath the surface.

Slamming her fist down on the console Joleen shouted, *"This did not need to happen! Those morons killed themselves!"* Then addressing Molly and Bonnie Mae, she apologetically stated; "What you just witnessed is what happens when the godless ally themselves with radical extremists. When catastrophe is inevitable, their capricious partnership crumbles, both parties ending up victims of their own selfishness. Do not feel bad girls, we gave them sufficient warning to leave these waters and they had no right whatsoever to fire their missiles in the first place! We will leave this up to the U.S. Military to sort out." Then turning to Corey she asked, "What direction are the currents pulling the debris field?"

He responded, "It is a bit hard to track in this storm, but it appears ... Northeasterly."

"Good; hopefully our caverns are safe. For now, we need to get back to the island and fill our people in on what is going on. There is no telling what consequences we will face if the results of this incident are traced back to us."

Chapter 26

The deep, wide, subterranean channel beneath the cliff was a welcome relief to Socrates and his friends, the brackish water sparkling clear and incredibly invigorating. Several hundred yards in, they discovered the unusual source of the flow, a fresh water spring bubbling up from a large fissure in the channel's limestone floor. Dozens of feet above the waterline, the domed ceiling supported beautiful, multi-colored stalactites of differing lengths, their glowing effervescence providing enough ambient light for complete visibility throughout the entire channel. In the distance, Amaya heard familiar laughter. She raced ahead to scout out the source and sure enough it was little Manny with his younger sibling Makoa, the two young plesiosaurs racing through the channel on a tear, breaching and diving, challenging each other with amazing acrobatics. When Manny spotted Amaya, he swept in beside her, pulling up short to engulf her in his wake. He then swam up to her with a big dumb smile on his face and asked, "What do you think; was that awesome or what?"

Amaya replied, "Yes, Manny, that was definitely awesome. But, how did you and your brother get here?"

"Well, my dad took a bunch of us to meet Kabooga. Boy, did he scare the krill out of us before showing us his garden with all his cool stuff. When everyone got ready to go back to the bay, dad took off fast. We were supposed to try to catch him, but Makoa and I decided to see where the big battle took place. We hid and waited a little while before asking Kabooga to take us there. He made us promise not to tell our pop. Wow, it must have been one big romp. We even saw remains of the crocs. Their teeth were *big*."

Just then, Socrates and the rest of their group caught up to Amaya, Socrates asking, "Where did these two come from?"

Amaya took a moment to explain, oblivious to the hidden danger lurking above. However, Mau was cruising in behind them, concerned about the possibility of other evil schemes the former captors could impose on unwary prey. His hunch was right; in an instant, six figures appeared on the rocks above the waterline, cutting ropes to towering spring loaded poles attached to a large net, instantly ensnaring Socrates and his friends and whisking them straight up out of the water. Mau let out a deafening roar while speeding forward and breaching high in the air, catching the edge of the net in his massive jaws, the overwhelming weight and vicious head shaking power of the fifty-foot plesiosaur causing the entire structure to collapse. Crashing down hard, the trap brought with it the six individuals responsible for setting it.

While Socrates was busy freeing his friends caught in the net, Mau focused on corralling the perpetrators, backing them up against a smooth limestone wall, making any chance of their escape impossible. Facing his enemies with eyes aflame with anger from their assault on his family and friends, Mau began slowly re-opening his jaws, exposing savage flesh-shredding teeth that were dancing with multicolored light reflecting off the causeway's ceiling. Rolling his head back and blaring out another ear-shattering roar, his attack was suddenly interrupted when Bondar breached out of the water between Mau and his prey.

The great plesiosaur was angry, retreating back beneath the surface and shouting; *"Get out of my way! These too have to die!"*

The Hammerhead replied, "I do not disagree, my friend. However, none of us are hurt. I think we should take them to our human escorts and let them determine their fate."

Mau's angry eyes terrified Bondar, the piscean giant gliding from side to side while slapping his great fins hard on the surface, magnifying the terror he was inflicting on his prey. Two Stars finally swam up to him, calming him with the words; "Please, listen to Bondar. Remember that we are a team. Look at these attackers as opposed to the one attacking the little boy."

Mau's prey was huddling up against the stone surface, shaking in fear, having nowhere to escape. Two Stars continued: "Let's get them back to the mouth of the cove and let the humans deal with them. Who knows, perhaps 'our catch' can help lure the real enemies into a trap *we* set."

Mau thought for a moment, finally nodding his approval of Two Stars' advice. He gave her a wink, turned toward his frightened prey and swooped in close with his mouth wide open, causing them to swim frantically back to the entrance to the causeway. He kept nudging them with his snout and slapping the surface with his paddle-like fins, playing with them as though their next stroke could be their last. Bondar urged Socrates and all of their friends to follow.

Chapter 27

Mau's mighty roar kept echoing through the subterranean passage like claps of angry thunder. Malanai and Rev, followed by Ben and their small band of recruits, hastened to find out what was going on, yielding plenty of space to Mau as he emerged from the channel herding his prey into the deeper water of the bay. Rev suddenly let out a challenging bellow, signaling Mau to back off. Mau complied to Rev's urging, but not before lowering his head and gnashing his teeth in the face of his opponents. Bondar and Two Stars then took their positions behind their victims, slowly swimming back and forth with fins slicing above the waterline to enforce their control.

The individuals in the water were shaking like leaves, a terrifying realization sweeping over them that they were someone's next meal. Malanai and Rev moved in closer to get a better look at who it was that Mau managed to capture. A tear started dribbling down Malanai's face upon recognizing the six individuals as some of her closest friends. They were the only ones who opposed her uncle's treatment of Ben and the other captives. It took a moment for Malanai to gather herself before asking; "What are you doing? You weren't teamed up with Logar, were you?"

One of the two women in the group cried out to Malanai, "No! Oh please Malanai believe us, we tried to help your brother Nasaur to resist Ashbon and his men. However, Nasaur had to flee for his life and is currently in hiding. We have no idea where he went and are now at the mercy of Ashbon. Since the battle in the bay most of our food sources have been so scarce that we were forced to follow Logar into the channel with the threat of being executed if we returned without food." Then, looking around at the band of freed captives all mounted up on seahorses, the young woman asked; "What is going on Malanai?"

Malanai instructed the Posse to get everyone to shore. Upon exiting the water, she urged Ben; "You and the others gather some food. My friends look famished."

With a puzzled look on his face Ben replied; *"You are going to believe their story just like that? I remember them dutifully serving your uncle before the big battle!"*

Malanai took him aside for a moment: "I know what it looked like at the time. However, who do you think it was that helped provide the ointment for your wounds every time you were whipped by the guards? These are my loyal friends and they are just as much victims of Ashbon's policy of dominance as you were to my uncle's. Believe me; I am sure they are as committed as we are to put this terroristic nonsense to rest ... *forever!"*

Socrates' small band of friends rallied around their leader in deep water several hundred feet from the shoreline, Two Stars asking him, "So, what now?"

Facing the shoreline Socrates thought for a moment with eyes stone cold, a steely grip of marked determination slowly sculpting the big cod's face, his brow furling, his lips slowly rolling back exposing rows of vicious sharp teeth. After a moment of silence his head whipped around, his voice stern and determined; "I do not know what our escorts are up against, but it appears the opposition is still viable. It is time we rally our forces and ... *finish* what we started!"

Coming Soon:

Beyond The Abyss – Book Five

Printed in the United States
By Bookmasters